I Can't Handle A Man Like Rex Tanner.

Yes, I can. And I will.

Rex's leather and outdoor scent enveloped her, and his nearness made her woozy. The temptation to discover how those long, slightly rough fingers would feel on her skin was a totally new experience and a step in the right direction...if Juliana found the courage to follow through with her plan.

"Why don't we get out of here?" Her words gushed out in a breathless invitation instead of the firm request she'd intended.

A bone-melting smile slanted Rex's lips. "That's the best offer I've had all night."

Dear heavens. She'd truly gone and bought herself a bad boy.

* * *

Don't miss
Exposing the Executive's Secrets, available in July,
and
Bending to the Bachelor's Will, coming in August,
from Emilie Rose and Silhouette Desire.

D0181081

Dear Reader,

Things are heating up in our family dynasty series, THE ELLIOTTS, with *Heiress Beware* by Charlene Sands. Seems the rich girl has gotten herself into a load of trouble and has ended up in the arms of a sexy Montana stranger. (Well...there are worse things that could happen.)

We've got miniseries galore this month, as well. There's the third book in Maureen Child's wonderful SUMMER OF SECRETS series, *Satisfying Lonergan's Honor,* in which the hero learns a startling fifteen-year-old secret. And our high-society continuity series, SECRET LIVES OF SOCIETY WIVES, features *The Soon-To-Be-Disinherited Wife* by Jennifer Greene. Also, Emilie Rose launches a brand-new trilogy about three socialites who use their trust funds to purchase bachelors at a charity auction. TRUST FUND AFFAIRS gets kicked off right with *Paying the Playboy's Price.*

June also brings us the second title in our RICH AND RECLUSIVE series, which focuses on wealthy, mysterious men. *Forced to the Altar,* Susan Crosby's tale of a woman at the mercy of a...yes...wealthy, mysterious man, will leave you breathless. And rounding out the month is Cindy Gerard's emotional tale of a pregnant heroine who finds a knight in shining armor with *A Convenient Proposition.*

So start your summer off right with all the delectable reads from Silhouette Desire.

Happy reading!

Melissa Jeglinski

Melissa Jeglinski
Senior Editor
Silhouette Books

Please address questions and book requests to:
Silhouette Reader Service
U.S.: 3010 Walden Ave., P.O. Box 1325, Buffalo, NY 14269
Canadian: P.O. Box 609, Fort Erie, Ont. L2A 5X3

EMILIE ROSE
Paying the Playboy's Price

Silhouette Desire

Published by Silhouette Books
America's Publisher of Contemporary Romance

If you purchased this book without a cover you should be aware
that this book is stolen property. It was reported as "unsold and
destroyed" to the publisher, and neither the author nor the
publisher has received any payment for this "stripped book."

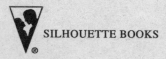 SILHOUETTE BOOKS

ISBN 0-373-76732-3

PAYING THE PLAYBOY'S PRICE

Copyright © 2006 by Emilie Rose Cunningham

All rights reserved. Except for use in any review, the reproduction
or utilization of this work in whole or in part in any form by any
electronic, mechanical or other means, now known or hereafter
invented, including xerography, photocopying and recording, or in
any information storage or retrieval system, is forbidden without
the written permission of the editorial office, Silhouette Books,
233 Broadway, New York, NY 10279 U.S.A.

All characters in this book have no existence outside the imagination of
the author and have no relation whatsoever to anyone bearing the same
name or names. They are not even distantly inspired by any individual
known or unknown to the author, and all incidents are pure invention.

This edition published by arrangement with Harlequin Books S.A.

® and TM are trademarks of Harlequin Books S.A., used under license.
Trademarks indicated with ® are registered in the United States Patent
and Trademark Office, the Canadian Trade Marks Office and in other
countries.

Visit Silhouette Books at www.eHarlequin.com

Printed in U.S.A.

Books by Emilie Rose

Silhouette Desire

Expecting Brand's Baby #1463
The Cowboy's Baby Bargain #1511
The Cowboy's Million-Dollar Secret #1542
A Passionate Proposal #1578
Forbidden Passion #1624
Breathless Passion #1635
Scandalous Passion #1660
Condition of Marriage #1675
Paying the Playboy's Price #1732

*Trust Fund Affairs

EMILIE ROSE

lives in North Carolina with her college-sweetheart husband and four sons. Writing is Emilie's third (and hopefully her last) career. She's managed a medical office and run a home day care, neither of which offers half as much satisfaction as plotting happy endings. Her hobbies include quilting, gardening and cooking (especially cheesecake). Her favorite TV shows include *ER*, *CSI* and Discovery Channel's medical programs. Emilie's a country music fan because she can find an entire book in almost any song.

Emilie loves to hear from her readers and can be reached at P.O. Box 20145, Raleigh, NC 27619 or at www.EmilieRose.com.

To the Black Sheep.
Long may we baa and may the pasture
always be as green.

One

"Is our uptight account auditor ready to be corrupted? Your bachelor's coming up next."

Juliana Alden downed her complimentary champagne with the grace of a beer-guzzling dock worker in hopes of drowning the second thoughts swarming around her midsection like angry bees. She discarded her glass on a passing waiter's tray and grabbed another for courage before facing Andrea and Holly, her two best friends and cohorts in tonight's foolhardy scheme.

"I've never felt more naked in my life. I will never grant the two of you carte blanche with my wardrobe again. My nightie covers more skin than this slip dress."

She yanked the thin strap of her dress back onto her shoulder *again,* and then tugged downward on the short hem, which barely covered her hips. Sneaking out the club's back door gained appeal with each passing second, but if she bolted Andrea and Holly would never forgive her. Then again, they were the ones responsible for garbing her in a dress that could send her father into cardiac arrest if he ventured out of the cigar room long enough to see it, so their opinions were suspect.

Andrea waved away her objections. "You have the figure for it and red is a great color on you. Don't wimp out now, Juliana."

A sea of screaming, nearly hysterical women surrounded them, bidding on the men being auctioned off in the name of charity with the same ferocity as the shark feeding frenzy Juliana had witnessed at a nearby aquarium. She'd bet her monthly pedicure the walls of the prestigious Caliber Club ballroom had never reverberated in quite the same way before. The pandemonium only increased her doubts about the plan the three of them had concocted over quesadillas and, clearly, one too many margaritas.

Praying for courage and finding none, Juliana took a deep breath and then another sip of champagne. What in the world had possessed her to believe she could cast off thirty years of being a Goody Two-shoes to bid on the baddest bachelor on the auction block tonight? She should have started with a smaller rebellion, but no, she'd chosen to launch a massive insurrection on her first attempt.

As an account auditor in her family's privately owned banking chain, she was cautious by nature. She worked a predictable job and drove a sensible sedan. She found comfort in following the rules, having her life add up in precise, orderly rows and in steadily ascending the career ladder the way her mother had before her.

But the sudden pressure to marry for the good of the company had shaken that ladder and made Juliana feel more like a commodity being bartered in the merger negotiations between Alden Bank and Trust and Wilson Savings and Loan than a human being.

"I can't believe I let you talk me into this. Maybe I'm not

ready for the tarnish-your-halo type of man. Perhaps I should choose someone a little less…" At a loss for words, she shrugged. How could she describe the man whose picture in the bachelor auction program had given her hot flashes?

"Studly?" Holly asked with a wicked grin.

Understatement of the year. Juliana nodded.

Bachelor number nine took the stage and Juliana's heart cha-chaed erratically. The crowd of usually dignified ladies hooted, whistled and stomped their expensively shod feet. If any man could tempt a woman to take a few risks and break a few rules, that one could. Looking completely at home in the spotlight, he flashed an I-dare-you grin and encouraged the already rowdy crowd to make more noise by clapping his hands and swinging his hips to the loud music like the head-lining performer he'd once been.

The man knew how to move. She'd grant him that. A shiver skipped down her spine.

His tight black T-shirt stretched across broad shoulders, molding a well-developed chest and encircling bulging biceps. Jeans, faded in those intriguing places she ought to be embarrassed to look at rode low on lean hips, and he wore cowboy boots—something you didn't see often in the port city of Wilmington, North Carolina. Given that every other man who'd crossed the stage before him tonight had worn a tux, the bar owner's casual attire screamed *renegade*—coinciden-tally, the name of his bar and the word emblazoned across the back of his shirt.

Juliana's pulse boomed so loudly she could barely hear the MC's long-winded introduction. Had the woman never heard the old cliché "silence is golden"? If she'd hush and let people *look* at Rex Tanner, then her job would do itself. What woman wouldn't want to be carried off in those muscle corded arms or be coerced by that naughty I'm-gonna-get-you smile?

"'Feel the power between your legs—one month of Harley and horseback-riding lessons,'" Andrea read aloud from the program. "Juliana, if this guy can't show you what you've been missing, then I'm going to check to see if you still have a pulse. He's exactly what you need to derail you from your mother's insane idea."

Juliana gulped the remainder of her drink. The bubbles burned her nose and brought tears to her eyes. "I'm still not convinced there's anything wrong with my mother's suggestion. Wally is a nice guy."

"You're not in love with him and he's boring," Holly stated.

"More effective than a sleeping pill," Andrea added. "And he's a pushover. You'd be wearing the pants in that relationship."

And that was a problem? The woman-in-charge role had worked for Juliana's parents. "I love you both for worrying about me and I understand your concerns, but logically, Wally is a good choice. He's steady, even-tempered and ambitious—like me—and he's the only man I've ever dated who understands the demands of my career and the hours it requires. We can talk for hours without an awkward silence."

Andrea snorted. "About work. What happens when that subject gets old or, God forbid, you're still with him when you retire? Are you going to discuss credits and debits in bed? I know you, Juliana. Once you commit to a job—or a marriage—you'll never give up on it. Forget logic for once in your life. This is your last chance to see that there can and *should* be more than convenience to a relationship."

Last chance. The phrase stuck in Juliana's head. Her last chance before agreeing to marry Wallace Wilson—son of the owner of the bank poised to merge with Alden's—in a sensible, but loveless match.

She shifted uneasily. Okay, maybe her friends had a point. Wally wasn't Mr. Excitement, but he was kind, pleasant-looking and steadfast. If she married him, they'd probably have predictable Saturday-night-duty sex for the next fifty years. On the other hand, routines were good and sex wasn't everything. It certainly shouldn't be the basis for something as important as marriage. Emotions were volatile and unpredictable. Similar ethics and mutual respect were far more important and dependable qualities. If she married Wally, they'd develop other shared interests and love would grow over time like a safe investment....

Wouldn't it?

Of course it would. If she had doubts, all she had to do was look at her parents. They'd married almost four decades ago to join two banking families, and they'd remained married when many of their friends had divorced.

The archway leading toward the exit drew her gaze again. Should she escape before diving off the bridge of sanity? No. A promise was a promise. But she truly hated going first. She turned back to her friends. "Swear to me you won't back out. You will buy bachelors tonight no matter what."

Holly and Andrea smiled angelically and raised their right hands as if taking the oath on a Bible. Juliana didn't trust those smiles. While her friends' lives might not be as methodically plotted out as hers, tonight's escapade was totally out of character for all three of them. Surely one of them would come to her senses before the evening ended?

The microphone screeched, jerking Juliana's attention back to the hunk commanding center stage—the one she'd been trying hard to ignore. How could any woman resist him? The man was a Grade-A gorgeous devil from his thick black ponytail to his worn low-heeled boots. He wouldn't need to read an instruction manual to know how to pleasure a woman—assuming that woman could be pleased.

But purchasing the cowboy's package would take more

than recklessness and champagne courage. It meant flagrantly disregarding her mother's wishes—something she'd carefully avoided until now for fear of the repercussions. But Juliana had to admit the proposed engagement combined with her thirtieth birthday had left her wondering if there was more to life. She'd promised Holly and Andrea she'd investigate the possibility before meekly agreeing to the future her mother had planned for her.

That didn't prevent Juliana from wondering if she'd taken on a bigger challenge than she could handle when she'd selected her bachelor—a man the complete opposite of anyone she'd dated in the past. She said a silent prayer that the rebel's price would exceed the limit she, Andrea and Holly had agreed upon, and then she could choose a less intimidating man.

Coward. If you do, then your plan will fail.

Her plan was beginning to sound more than a little like tequila madness. For once in her life, Juliana had decided to break the rules and, since she didn't have the first clue where to start, she'd chosen Rex Tanner, a hell-raising rebel who she hoped would lead her astray. For the next month, she'd put herself in his corrupting hands and then once she had this last fling out of the way and she was certain she wasn't missing out on anything worthwhile, she could marry Wally with no regrets.

"Go home before you get into trouble."

Juliana nearly tumbled off her flimsy sandals at her bossy older brother's growled warning. She refused to admit she'd like nothing more than to turn and run as fast as her heels would carry her. To annoy Eric, she raised her numbered fan, offering the first bid on Mr. Too-Hot-To-Handle.

Andrea and Holly grinned and gave her thumbs-up. Juliana didn't dare glance across the room to where her mother, the charity event's chief organizer, watched with an eagle eye.

She tilted her head back to glare at her brother. "How much trouble can a month of riding lessons cause? Go away, Eric."

"I'm not worried about the horseback-riding lessons because you already know how to ride. It's the other half of the prize that concerns me. You'll kill yourself on a motorcycle. Be reasonable, Juliana. You are not the most coordinated person on the planet."

The barb stung—mostly because it was true. In fact, these days she limited her exercise routine to swimming because then she wouldn't fall off anything and get hurt when her mind strayed to work issues.

Eric attempted to take her numbered paddle, but Juliana snatched it out of his reach and stabbed it into the air. "I'm thirty years old—too old for you to be telling me what to do."

"Somebody needs to. You and your friends—" he glared at Holly and Andrea "—must have been out of your minds to come up with this plan. Buying men, for crissakes. If you want to support the charity, buy Wallace and not this—"

"Hunk," Holly interrupted, earning a scowl from Eric.

Juliana pasted on the placating smile she reserved for difficult customers. "Actually, Eric, our mother came up with the bachelor-auction idea. Andrea, Holly and I are merely supporting her efforts."

"Dammit, Juliana, you can't handle a guy like him. He'll chew you up and spit you out. Use your brain. Buy Wally. He's...*safe*." He snatched at Juliana's fan again and once more she jerked it away.

Safe. Those four letters said it all. She'd played it safe her entire life and where had that gotten her? Ahead in her career, but pathetically far behind in her personal life. She'd never fallen head over heels in love or even lust, and she couldn't help wondering if she was capable of such intense emotions. Not that she wanted the heartache, but was it too much to ask for bells, whistles and earth-moving orgasms? For a woman like her—one who trusted cold, hard facts more than fickle emotions? Probably. But for once in her life, she didn't want to play it safe.

She glanced at the man on the stage. *Safe* didn't make her skin tingle or her breath quicken. She shoved the paddle into the air this time holding it high above her head and slightly behind her. Her brother was taller, but he was as conservative as she was. He wouldn't make a scene or wrestle her to the ground to keep her from bidding.

"I don't want to buy Wally. Saturday-night suppers? How unimaginative is that? Besides, I already have a standing dinner date with him on Fridays. What's wrong with having a little fun? You should try it sometime."

And then she winced. Eric had been very publicly jilted a few months ago and fun was probably the last thing on his mind. She suspected his heart hadn't been broken, but his pride had to have taken a serious blow. The worst part was that since he'd failed to marry into the Wilson banking family, her mother had decided Juliana should.

She waved her paddle—a little more desperately this time. "Eric, I have carefully thought this out, and I know what I'm doing, so leave me alone."

"*Sold* to number 223," the MC shouted from the stage. "Pay up and collect your prize, young lady."

Juliana's stomach plunged to her crimson-painted toenails. She looked from Eric to her mother's horrified expression. Andrea and Holly clapped and cheered. Juliana didn't need to double-check her number to know she'd won the rebel, and she had no idea how much she'd paid for him—a true shock for someone who tracked money for a living. Slowly lowering her arm, she swallowed and briefly closed her eyes as a bolt of unadulterated panic zigzagged through her. She wasn't ready to face the stage and the consequences of her virgin voyage into mutiny. She might never be ready.

Dizziness forced her to inhale. She faked a smile for Eric and anyone else who might be watching. "Thank you for your concern, big brother, but aren't you supposed to be behind the curtain getting ready for your turn on the block?"

Eric flinched and paled. A smidgen of guilt pricked Juliana for verbally jabbing his sore spot with a deliberate taunt. Her brother was not happy their mother had shanghaied him as a bachelor. But Eric wasn't Juliana's problem right now. She had her own catastrophe-in-the-making to handle. Dread ballooned inside her.

With her brother's muttered curses and Andrea and Holly's "Go get 'ems" ringing in her ears, Juliana made her way to the table in the corner of the room and handed over her check to collect her…*gulp*…prize.

Her mother, with fury in her eyes, met her there. "Juliana Alden, are you out of your mind? And where in the world did you find that disgraceful dress?"

Juliana's insides clenched tighter as all her doubts ambushed her at once. She *must* have been temporarily insane to agree to Andrea's suggestion that they celebrate their thirtieth birthdays by spending part of their trust funds on something wild, wicked and totally selfish.

No, not insane. Desperate. If she couldn't feel the heart-pounding passion other women whispered about with a man as blatantly sexy as the rebel, then she was a lost cause, and she'd be better off with a man like Wally who wouldn't expect more than she could deliver.

But while Juliana admired her mother's business acumen and hoped to emulate Margaret Alden's career success, the two of them had never been close, so confessing the tangle of emotions driving her decision wasn't a viable option.

"Mother, I have always done everything you've ever asked of me, but tonight, this—*he*—is for me."

She glanced beyond her mother's shoulder. Juliana's prize stalked toward her in long purposeful strides, and the hairs on her neck rose. Why did she feel like cornered prey? Determined not to be cowed by the cocky challenge in his eyes, she assumed the debutante pose her mother had drilled into her— tall and regal, chin high—and hoped her knees weren't visibly knocking beneath her scandalously short hem.

From a distance of ten yards—and closing far too quickly—the rebel's dark gaze drifted over her, making her intensely aware that she wore nothing but a thong beneath the thin dress.

Had she ever met a man who oozed this much sexuality? Definitely not. Her pulse fluttered irregularly and her skin tightened and warmed.

"What about Wallace?" her mother whispered angrily.

With great effort, Juliana tore her gaze away from her prize and refocused on her mother. "I will very likely spend the rest of my life with Wally. Neither of you should begrudge me a month of riding lessons."

Her mother's lips flattened. "One month and then I fully expect you to come to your senses. The Wilsons are a fine family and Wallace has impeccable manners." Her mother could be describing a pedigreed pooch, but then her mother would probably prefer a well-trained lap dog to a real man. "Be assured your father won't be as understanding."

No, he definitely would not. He'd be whatever her mother told him to be. As much as Juliana loved her father, she wasn't blind to his faults.

"Hey, babe." The deep gravelly voice sent goose bumps parading over Juliana's skin. She ignored her mother's shocked gasp and faced the man who'd come to a halt a yard away. The heat in his naughty smile and coffee-colored eyes robbed the strength from Juliana's knees. He offered his hand. "I'm Rex and I'm going to teach you to ride."

Ride what? Or whom? The questions popped involuntarily into her head and she couldn't breathe. Her teeth met with an audible click when she closed her mouth. She had definitely bitten off more of a challenge than she could chew. Rex Tanner was bigger, sexier and far more intimidating up close than he'd been onstage or in the tiny two-inch picture printed in the program. Even in her heels, Juliana's eyes barely reached the level of his mouth. What a mouth. And boy, did he look like he knew how to use it.

That is what you wanted, isn't it?

No. Yes. No. Ohmigod, Eric was right. I can't handle a man like Rex Tanner.

Yes, I can. And I will.

The corners of his lips quirked upward as if he were used to dumbstruck females.

Embarrassed, Juliana pasted on a polite smile. Her fingers trembled as she slid her hand into Rex's. "Hello, Rex. I'm Juliana."

Warm, callused skin abraded her palm as he grasped her hand, and when he slid his other arm around her shoulders, pulled her closer and turned her toward the photographer, every cell in Juliana's body screeched in alarm at the searing press of his flesh against her side and his long fingers curved over her bare shoulder.

"Smile, babe," he whispered in a voice as rough and piercing as a rusty nail. She felt the impact deep in her womb.

His leather-and-outdoors scent enveloped her, and his nearness made her woozy. She blamed the stars in her eyes on the camera's flash and knew she lied.

As soon as Octavia Jenkins, the newspaper reporter

covering the event, and her photographer sidekick departed, Juliana quickly disengaged and scrambled to make order out of her chaotic response. The temptation to discover how those long, slightly rough fingers would feel on the rest of her skin was a totally new experience and a step in the right direction *if* she found the courage to follow through with her plan.

If? You have planned this for weeks. You are absolutely committed to following through. No backing out now.

Overly conscious of her mother's disapproval and the stares of the other patrons aimed at them, Juliana met Rex's gaze.

"Why don't we get out of here?" Her words gushed out in a breathless invitation instead of the firm request she'd intended.

A bone-melting smile slanted his lips. "That's the best offer I've had all night."

After delivering a lengthy, censuring look, her mother pivoted and stormed off in a regal huff. Juliana turned in the opposite direction and headed for the exit before she could turn coward and ask for her money back. Without looking over her shoulder, she knew Rex Tanner followed. She could feel him behind her, hear the rhythmic thud of his boots on the marble floor, see the jealous glares of the women they passed directed toward her and the appreciative appraisals aimed at him. Many of those women were married and some were old enough to be his mother.

Rex reached past her to push open the club's front door, and a blast of sobering air smacked Juliana's face as she stepped outside.

Dear heavens. She'd bought herself a bad boy.

What was she going to do with him?

And how far was she willing to let this experiment go?

Bought by a spoiled rich chick with more money than sense. Rex studied Juliana's arrogant bearing and questioned his sanity in agreeing to his sister's crazy suggestion to use the bachelor auction to publicize his bar. If the bank note weren't coming due in sixty days, then nothing could have persuaded him to get back on a stage in front of screaming women.

Been there. Done that. Burned by it.

Self-disgust didn't stop him from appreciating the tasty morsel in front of him as she swished her red-wrapped hips away from the noise and chaos inside. Her lingerie-style dress looked like something she'd wear to bed instead of to a swanky country club, and the dark curtain of hair bouncing between her shoulder blades glowed with the same rich patina of his old guitar.

For the first time since moving to Wilmington, he found himself attracted to a woman, but everything about Juliana, from her cultured southern voice to her expensive clothing and the chunk of change she'd dropped on him tonight, screamed money. Rich gals like her didn't settle for rough-off-the-ranch guys like him long-term, and he'd had enough meaningless encounters to last a lifetime. When he'd left Nashville and the groupies behind, he'd sworn he'd never use or be used by a woman again. As long as Juliana realized that she'd bought his auction package and nothing else, they'd get along fine. But before he followed her wherever she was headed, he needed to be certain of one thing.

"Hey, Juli," he called as they reached the semicircular stairs leading down to the parking lot.

She jerked to a halt and spun to face him. Her bright blue eyes nearly made him forget what he was going to say.

Her chin inched upward. "My name is Juliana."

Stuck-up or not, she didn't look like the kind of woman who had to buy men. "Yeah, sure. You have a jealous husband who'll be gunning for me?"

A confused frown puckered her brows. "A husband?"

"The guy trying to stop you from bidding," he clarified.

"That was my brother. I'm not married."

"'S'all right then as long as you're over twenty-one."

Her long lashes fluttered and a pleat formed between her eyebrows. "You have jealous husbands chasing you?"

She'd ignored his comment about age. "Not anymore."

Her red lips parted and her chest—a damned fine chest—rose. "But you did?"

"Yeah." Most guys didn't take it well when they found out their wives had slept with another man. Rex hadn't taken the news that some of the groupies were married well, either—especially since the info had often been delivered via their husbands' fists after the intimate encounters.

He thought he heard Juliana wheeze as she turned to descend the steps. He'd have to be dead not to appreciate her long, sleek and sexy-as-all-get-out legs atop those red heels. She stopped abruptly at the base of the stairs with a distressed expression on her pretty face.

"Problem?"

She touched long slender fingers to her temple and then against her throat. "I rode with friends. I don't have a car, and I want to…" She looked past his shoulder and panic flared in her eyes.

He turned and spotted the pearl-clad dragon lady who'd organized the event and an uptight-looking man coming through the front door of the club. Understanding dawned. "You want to get out of here?"

"Yes, and fast."

"Did you write a bad check?"

Impossible as it seemed, her regal posture turned even starchier, as if he'd insulted her. "Of course not. Please, get me out of here."

These days he avoided ugly scenes. "My bike's this way."

Her eyes nearly popped out of her head. She gestured to her skimpy attire. "I'm hardly dressed for a motorcycle ride."

He ought to leave her, but dammit, he'd agreed to this stupid auction and he would follow through. Besides, he wouldn't wish the dragon lady on anybody. "I don't see any taxis. If you need to make a fast getaway, then I'm your only option. Where to? Home?"

She grimaced. "Anywhere but there."

"Let's go." He grabbed her elbow and towed her toward his Harley. She jogged to keep up. When they reached the side of his motorcycle—one of a handful of items he'd kept from his past—he tossed her his spare helmet and waited to see that she knew how to fasten it before donning his own. "Hop on and hold on."

Seconds later she'd mounted the bike behind him and gingerly clutched his waist, but she kept several inches between them. He twisted the throttle. The engine roared and the bike surged forward as he released the clutch. Her squeal pierced the deep growl of the Harley, and then her arms banded around him with close to rib-cracking force, erasing the gap between them.

Big mistake. Having her naked legs wrapped around his hips with the heat of her crotch pressed snugly against his butt just might melt a few brain cells. And if he couldn't ignore the softness of her breasts mashing against his shoulder blades and concentrate on the road, then he'd end up wrapping the bike around a telephone pole.

Warm, humid air rushed past them, fluttering her short skirt and baring more of her toned thighs. He forced his eyes away from the tantalizing sight and back on the road. Where could he take her? The shorter the ride, the better. The roar of the engine made asking impossible. Might as well take her to his place since he and Juliana needed to compare calendars and set up the riding lessons.

Pride filled his chest as Renegade's lights came into view. He'd bought the vacant riverfront building in the historical district eight months ago. It had taken a lot of sweat and most of his cash to turn the downstairs into a business and the upstairs into a home his sister Kelly and her girls could visit. He'd opened his doors four months ago, but business hadn't been as brisk as he'd hoped—hence his participation in the auction.

He pulled into his narrow private driveway, automatically counting the empty parking spaces out front as he passed. If he wanted to stay in Wilmington near his sister, then he had to turn a profit soon and pay off the bank note.

He parked, climbed from the bike and removed his helmet. Juliana remained seated. She fumbled to unfasten her chin strap and then pulled off her helmet. Rex rocked back on his heels with a silent whistle of admiration. Now there was a centerfold-quality picture—minus the staples—guaranteed to keep a man up all night. Mile-long legs straddling the Harley's black seat, red strappy heels, skimpy dress, beautiful face, tumbled hair. A hot package.

But good-looking women had caused him plenty of trouble before, so he tamped down his physical response and offered his hand. Gingerly, she curled her soft fingers around his and then struggled to draw her leg over the seat. A glimpse of her candy apple–red panties hit his belly like a fireball.

He caught her elbow as she wobbled on her heels on the cobblestone sidewalk. The evening breeze plastered the silky fabric of her dress against her puckered nipples. Was she wearing anything besides those panties under there? His pulse revved faster. *Forget it, Tanner.*

She scrubbed her arms and her tiny silver purse sparkled in the streetlights like rhinestones under stage lights. "Could we go inside?"

He motioned for her to precede him. When he reached past her to open the door, her scent, an intoxicating mixture of flowers and spice, filled his lungs. She stepped inside and looked around.

What did she think of his place? He'd played on Wilmington's TV and film industry. The bar's theme was movie rebels and renegades—men Rex had identified with back when he'd been a teen who couldn't wait to break free from family ranching tradition. He'd escaped the day he'd turned eighteen but, seventeen years later, the guilt of his bitter parting words still haunted him.

The bar itself took up most of the back wall. He'd filled the floor with tables—too many of which were empty on a Saturday night. The waitresses leaned against the back wall.

"You don't have any memorabilia from your music career in here."

The comment stopped him in his tracks. Juliana knew who he was even though he'd deliberately excluded his recent past in the auction bio. Had she bought him for the braggin' rights of bedding Rex Tanner, former Nashville bad boy? She wouldn't be the first with that goal. And as appealing as the idea of hitting the sheets with Juliana might be, he didn't want his old life intruding here. "No."

Her assessing gaze landed on him. "Wouldn't it be wise to trade on what people know of you?"

And be known as a has-been for the rest of his life? No thanks. "My music career is over. If people want a honky-tonk they can go elsewhere. Can I get you a drink?"

"No, thank you. May I stay here for an hour or so? As soon as the auction ends, I can call a friend for a ride."

"I'll take you home after we schedule your lessons." Her eyes widened. "I have a truck if you don't want to get back on the bike."

"Thank you, but I think I'll stay with one of my girlfriends tonight. She can come and get me. My car is at her place anyway. We rode to the auction together."

Why would a rich chick need to hide? She looked over the age of consent, but looks could be deceiving. "How old did you say you were?"

She hesitated. "I didn't say, but I'm thirty, if you must know. Didn't your mother ever teach you that it's rude to ask?"

His mother had taught him a lot of things. And like an ungrateful SOB, he'd thrown her lessons back in her face. "Aren't you a little old to be running away from home?"

"You don't understand. My parents…" She trailed off and took an anxious peek over his shoulder as if she expected them to burst through the door. "They won't understand about tonight."

"I don't have to know the whole story to know running's not going to solve anything." A lesson he'd learned the hard way.

"But—"

He held up a hand. "And I don't want to know the whole story. I'm here to give you riding lessons. That's it."

How did she manage to look down her nose at him when she was a good six to eight inches shorter than he was? "Fine."

He considered leaving her at the bar and going to his apartment to get his calendar, but she and her sexy dress had already caught the attention of the guys in the back corner. The men were regulars, friends of his deployed brother-in-law, and Rex didn't want anything to happen that would keep them from coming back. "Upstairs."

He waved to Danny, and pointed toward the private entrance leading to his apartment. From the wiseass smirk on his manager's face, Danny probably thought the boss was about to get laid. The thought sent a Roman candle of heat through Rex's veins. He doused it. He'd dodged every advance thrown his way since opening, and he wasn't about to get sucked into that drainpipe now.

Rex pulled his keys from his pocket, unlocked the door and motioned for Juliana to precede him up the stairs. If she wanted more than Harley and horseback-riding lessons from him, then she'd be disappointed.

Two

Who'd have guessed that after all these years of not getting hot and bothered that she could get turned on by something mechanical? Although Juliana suspected the motorcycle ride wasn't entirely to blame for her discombobulation.

"Have a seat." Rex prowled around the den of his apartment flicking on lamps to reveal a very masculine decor of cappuccino-colored leather and dark wood. The furniture looked expensive but not new. Relics from his days at the top of the country-music charts?

Juliana perched on the edge of the sofa tallying sensations and classifying the wide range of emotions she'd experienced tonight. *Safe* wasn't among them. She had an inkling this might be the beginnings of lust, but she couldn't be sure.

Fingers of wind had ripped at her clothing and tried to pull her off the bike when Rex had raced the motorcycle down a long, straight section of road. The scream bubbling in her throat had been caused by terror mixed with a smidgen of excitement. Each time he'd leaned into a curve, her heart had pounded so hard she'd thought it would explode. He'd probably have bruises tomorrow from where she'd clutched him so tightly. By the time they'd arrived at Renegade she'd practically burrowed under his skin.

And she'd liked it there.

Rex's abs had been steady and rock-hard beneath her knotted fingers, and the rough texture of jeans had abraded the sensitive skin of her inner thighs and the tender flesh between her legs. The heat of his broad back had seeped through his T-shirt and her thin dress to warm her breasts more effectively than any caress she'd ever experienced. When he'd climbed from the bike, her legs had been too weak to follow. In fact, they still hadn't quit shaking.

Which caused her extreme reaction? Fear or physical attraction? She didn't have much experience with either. In the past, she'd always been drawn by a man's intelligence more than his physique, but her reaction to Rex had nothing to do with his brain. She hated to admit she was shallow enough to look forward to exploring this new terrain.

He sat beside her on the sofa, opened a calendar on the coffee table and then angled to face her. The outside seam of his jeans scraped her knee and thigh. A shiver worked its way to the pit of her stomach and settled there like a hot rock.

"I usually work nights, so your lessons will have to be late mornings or on my days off. Which works for you?" The flirtatiousness he'd displayed at the auction disappeared behind a no-nonsense businesslike demeanor. Since she was counting on him to lead her astray, that wasn't a desirable development.

"I work weekdays."

"Doing what?"

With him sitting this close and holding her gaze that way,

Juliana had a hard time remembering what consumed most of her week. His scent and proximity had the oddest effect on her ability to think clearly. Funny, she lived for her job... What was it again? Oh, yes. "I'm an account auditor with Alden Bank and Trust."

His narrowed gaze traveled slowly from her face to her bare shoulders, over her dress and then her legs. Her body reacted as if he'd touched her by tightening, liquefying.

So this was animal attraction? She'd heard others talk about it, but she'd never experienced the sensation. She wanted to pick it apart and study the components the way she would account entries during an audit. Flushed skin. A tingle in her veins. Accelerated heart rate. Dampened palms.

"You don't look like any bean counter I've ever met." His skeptical expression robbed the words of any compliment and hit a sore spot. After earning an MBA from the local university, Juliana had accepted a position in the family bank's home office. She'd had to work doubly hard to prove her worth and quiet the rumors of nepotism, and she'd been proving herself ever since. But this wasn't work. She wanted Rex to see her as a desirable woman, not as a highly credentialed bank auditor.

"I've always been good with numbers." She downplayed. It was people skills she lacked. Growing up, her brother had been the socially adept one who'd held the titles of class president, homecoming king and every other desirable position. Juliana had been an ugly duckling who'd preferred books and horses to people. Andrea and Holly had been, and still were, her only close friends.

Rex thumped a beat on the table with his pen, drawing her attention back to his big, rough and scarred workman's hands. She'd listened to his music and it amazed her that such strong, masculine hands could pluck a guitar so beautifully.

"We'll meet after you get off work on Mondays and Thursdays, my days off. That'll give us a couple of hours of daylight."

She caught herself watching his lips move, blinked and refocused on his eyes—dark, knowing eyes that seemed to look right inside her.

"I've leased a smaller bike for you," he continued, "but you can't drive it until you've earned your motorcycle learner's permit and mastered a few basic skills."

The unexpected turn of the conversation pulled her from her corporeal exploration. "A learner's permit?"

"Required by North Carolina law. I'll give you the booklet tonight. Start studying. You'll have to take a written test at the Department of Motor Vehicles."

Her prize package required her to take a test? That hadn't been in the fine print, and she *always* read the fine print. "I work fifty to sixty hours a week. When am I supposed to find time to study and take a test?"

"Before the end of the month—unless you want the newspaper to report that you couldn't pass."

Her competitive instincts stirred. She hadn't taken a driving test in fifteen years, but she'd always been an excellent student. "Fine. Twice a week at six o'clock for four weeks."

"I'll let the reporter know." He closed the calendar and planted his hands on his knees. "Listen, Juliana, Renegade needs all the publicity it can get out of the newspaper series. You might not have noticed but the place isn't packed."

"I noticed. Business accounts are a large part of my job. Empty tables mean reduced revenue and reduced revenue means—"

He leaned toward her. Her mind went blank and her heart leaped in anticipation. She snatched a quick breath, wet her lips and lifted her mouth, but Rex didn't kiss her. Instead he dragged a fluffy pink boa and a small pink purse from beneath his sofa cushion and sat back again.

She blinked in surprise. *Had she bought a cross-dresser?* "Yours?" she squeaked.

The rugged lines of his face softened and his eyes warmed, turning her insides to mush. "My nieces'."

Shock receded. The rebel had nieces. And judging from his expression, he had a soft spot in his heart for them. The idea of using him to further her um...*physical* education had been a lot easier when she'd believed him to be one-hundred-percent bad boy, a heartless seducer of innocents, a man who'd get the job done and not think twice about it. Now the images of reckless rebel, concerned business owner and doting uncle tangled in a confusing mass in her head. But instead of turning her off, the combination intrigued her and made her want to know more. Not a good idea since this was a short-term project.

He stood and tossed the dress-up items into a wicker basket in the corner. "Let me make one thing clear. You bought horseback and Harley riding lessons and you're going to get them. But riding lessons are all I'm offering."

Half-dozen heartbeats later, his meaning sank in. Mortification burned over her skin like a desert wind. Was she so transparent? He couldn't know that she wondered how he'd kiss, how he'd taste and, more specifically, how she'd react to his embrace. Could he?

She wobbled to her feet. "I—I appreciate your candor."

"You ready to call for your ride yet?"

He couldn't wait to get rid of her. How embarrassing. Had she ever had a date so eager to show her the door? "Certainly."

The evening was not going as she'd anticipated and she had no idea how to get it back on track. What did she know about seduction? She'd counted on him doing all the work.

Why hadn't she developed a backup plan?

* * *

"So is he as great as he looks or is he all beauty, brawn and no brains?" Holly asked as Juliana climbed into her friend's Jeep outside Renegade.

"He's not just a pretty face." His dedication to his nieces and his business savvy in using the auction and the monthlong newspaper coverage as advertising proved Rex was more than an empty-headed pretty boy. "Did you get your firefighter?"

Holly abruptly reached for the radio and flipped through the stations. "No."

The rat. Had she and Andrea chickened out after sending Juliana into the bidding wars like a sacrificial lamb? "You promised you'd buy him."

"No, I promised I'd buy *a bachelor* and I did. The firefighter went for more money than we agreed upon—although *you* certainly broke that rule, didn't you? Besides, Eric was desperate."

Juliana recoiled. "Eric! *My brother, Eric?*"

Holly darted a glance in her direction and nodded.

"You cheated."

"No, I didn't. I wanted a man who would give me candlelit dinners and take me dancing. Eric's package promises Eleven Enchanted Evenings."

Juliana didn't like the blissful smile on Holly's face—not in connection to her brother. "But it's *Eric.*"

"So?"

"You wanted romance. Eric is no Prince Charming to your Cinderella. I'm having really icky thoughts of my brother kissing you good night, and I don't want to go there." She shuddered.

"I know you don't want to believe it, Juliana, but Eric is as much of a hunk as your rebel."

"Ick. Ick." She stuck her fingers in her ears. No matter what her friend said, Holly had cheated by taking the safe way out.

She unplugged her ears. "You and Andrea convinced me to go out on a limb and buy Rex. There is no risk involved in buying someone you know. Did Andrea also turn coward? Who did she buy?"

"Clayton."

Sympathy squeezed Juliana's heart and she sighed. "So she's really going through with it, then?"

"That's what she said." Holly didn't sound any happier about the situation than Juliana.

"I hope he doesn't break her heart again."

"I hope your rebel doesn't break yours. Those were some serious sparks between you when he walked you out."

Sparks? One-sided sparks, maybe. Rex Tanner didn't seem the least bit interested in fanning the flames Juliana could feel licking at her toes. At the moment, she had no idea how she'd change his mind, but given what she knew of his past, it shouldn't be too difficult.

"You are completely off base with that observation, my friend, and my heart will be just fine, thank you. Remember, my time with Rex Tanner is limited. He'd never fit in with my long-term career goals, and I seriously doubt an anal-retentive bank auditor whose idea of adventure is trying a new shade of nail polish would fit in with his."

Rex peeled his gaze from Juliana's behind for the fifth time and shook his head. Jodhpurs. He should have expected as much from a high-society chick who wrote five-figure checks without blinking.

"Next time wear jeans." Her formal riding attire was a far cry from Saturday night's scanty, sexy dress, but her jodhpurs looked as if they'd been spray painted over the luscious curve of her butt, and her sleeveless cotton blouse conformed to the shape of her breasts like a lover's hands. She'd pulled her shiny hair back with a clip and perched one of those prissy black velvet hard hats on her head—the kind horse-jumping folks wore. The siren-red nail polish was gone and so was most of her makeup. She looked better without the war paint. And why was he noticing? Her smooth skin had nothing to do with riding lessons.

"The boots are okay, and I can live with the hat."

"Please stop. Your flattery will turn my head," she replied with a hint of sarcasm, making him wonder if he'd read her lingering glances wrong Saturday night. "If I can find the time, I'll buy some jeans before Thursday."

He paused with the saddle midair. "You don't own a pair of jeans?"

"No. Casual Friday at the bank never gets that casual. You certainly have a lot of requirements for this package that weren't included in the description listed in the program."

"Most of it's common sense." He settled the saddle and saddle pad on Jelly Bean, the palomino mare he'd bought for his nieces. "Putting on a western saddle is similar to an English one. Here's how you secure it."

After demonstrating, he unfastened everything and stepped back. "Your turn."

Juliana tackled the task, but the mare tended to be lazy on hot summer afternoons. She bloated her stomach to prevent the tightening of the cinch around her belly. Juliana lacked the strength to make Jelly Bean exhale.

Positioning himself behind her, the way he did with the girls, he reached around to help her pull the leather strap. Having his arms around an attractive woman made his veins hum. He tried to ignore it. Unlike with his petite three- and five-year-old nieces, Juliana's taller frame lined up against his like a spoon in a drawer. Or a lover in bed. The mare shifted, bumping Juliana and her tightly wrapped behind against him.

Within seconds, her pants weren't the only tight ones. Rex steadied her and then stepped back, putting several yards and the hitching post between them. "Try the bridle next."

Juliana definitely knew her way around a horse. She rested the mare's muzzle against her breasts while she eased the bridle over her ears and brushed her forelock out of her eyes, and then she rewarded Jelly Bean for cooperating with a stroke down her golden neck and a scratch between her perked up ears.

He envied the horse being pressed between Juliana's breasts. Unacceptable. The auditor was off-limits. "Mount up."

She lifted her foot a couple of feet off the ground until the pull of fabric across her hips restricted her movements, and then she put her boot back down and looked at him over her shoulder. "Would you give me a leg up?"

Was there more than a legitimate request for help in her words? A tentative smile quivered on her lips—nothing seductive about it. In fact, he'd swear he saw nervousness in her eyes.

Get over yourself, Tanner. What does it say about your ego that you suspect every woman you meet of trying to get into your pants?

"Sure." As he did with the girls, he clasped Juliana's waist and lifted. Bad move. He didn't need to know that her waist was tiny or that her body heat would penetrate the thin fabric of her pants. He yanked his hands free so quickly Jelly Bean— the calmest horse he'd ever encountered—spooked and side-stepped. Rex lunged forward again, expecting Juliana to fall off, but she grabbed the saddle horn and managed to stay on.

"Is this another test?" More sarcasm. Okay, he'd definitely read her wrong.

She shifted in the saddle, and then stood in the stirrups and sank back down. She repeated the motion a couple of times. "This saddle feels odd, but comfortable."

Tugging at the suddenly tight collar of his T-shirt, he

looked away, cleared his throat and shifted his stance to ease the pinch of his jeans. The last time he'd seen a woman move like that, she'd been riding *him*. How long ago had that been? Too long. And hell, he couldn't remember her name or what she'd looked like.

There had been a lot of nameless encounters in his past— not something he was proud of now, but at the time he'd been floating on a wave of fame, taking the women who fell at his feet for granted and using them to make himself believe he was finally somebody. He'd been somebody all right. *Somebody stupid.*

His bandmates had used booze or drugs to come down from a post-performance high. Rex had used women—a practice that now disgusted him. He was damned lucky his carousing hadn't landed him in the morgue or given him an STD the way his father had predicted. Most of Rex's father's lectures had gone in one ear and out the other, but thank God the safe-sex one had stuck.

Rex had had a lucky escape, and he planned to put his sordid past behind him in a new city with a new career. He'd be the kind of brother he should have been to Kelly and an uncle Kelly's girls would be proud to claim. With their father deployed overseas, they needed someone they could depend on when their mom needed help.

Back to business. "The seat of a western saddle is deeper than an English one. It conforms to your shape." *And a damned fine shape it is.* "Take the reins in your hand with only one finger between them."

She did as he instructed, but looked unsure.

"Western horses move away from pressure and they prefer slack reins," he explained.

She stared down at him with a doubtful expression. "If my reins are slack how am I going to control the horse?"

"Use a soft touch. Your fingers and wrist work the bit, and rely on leg cues more than the bridle." Which drew his attention back to the length of her legs and the curve of her butt. If he didn't get his brain out of his briefs, she could get hurt. That kind of publicity wouldn't help the bar. "You know how to use leg cues?"

"Yes."

"Then signal her to walk."

Jelly Bean started forward. Rex kept pace beside them. A light evening breeze carried Juliana's perfume downwind, filling his lungs with her scent every time he inhaled.

He cursed his uncharacteristic distraction. Usually, he had tunnel vision. He saw what needed doing and didn't waver from his set course. His career and the destruction of it were perfect examples. He'd wanted to make it to the top and he had, and then, after his parents had died, he'd wanted out, but contracts had held him prisoner. Before leaving Nashville, he'd made sure he'd burned all his bridges. He shook his head to clear it. *Focus.*

"What's wrong?" she asked.

"Your motion. You're perching on top of the saddle instead of sinking into it, and every one of your muscles is strung as tight as a bow. Relax your upper body and your legs. Slump into the saddle."

"All my life I've been taught to sit up straight, and you're telling me to slouch?" Her haughty tone was exactly what he needed to remind himself of the differences between them.

"Not exactly, but you have to relax here." He quickly tapped the base of her spine with a fingertip. "Here." He nudged her thigh with his knuckle. "And here." His palm brushed her lower abdomen. He quickly withdrew it. Her body heat scalded his skin. He stepped away from the horse and crossed to the center of the riding ring. Ten yards wasn't enough distance to douse the fire smoldering in his gut.

"Cue her to jog when you're ready." Juliana nudged Jelly Bean into a slightly faster gait. Juliana tried to post, rising and lowering in the saddle from her knees as she would if riding English. "No posting. Sit."

She did and probably rattled a brain cell or two as she—and her perfectly shaped breasts—bounced along.

Rex ground his molars. He'd been attracted to a lot of women, but not this way. Had to be because he knew this relationship—like the ones in his past—would go nowhere. Falling back into old, bad habits was not part of his plan. "Scoot."

"Wh-at do you m-ean sc-oot?" The jarring broke her words into fragments. The mare snorted her displeasure.

"Rock your hips from the waist down." She looked at him as if he'd asked her to fly. In frustration he said, "Match your moves to the horse's. Like you're with your lover."

Her lips parted and her cheeks turned the color of a ripe peach. She jerked her face forward to stare straight between Jelly Bean's ears, but within seconds she had the correct motion. "Sorry. It's been a while, but I think I have it now."

Been a while? Riding a horse or with a lover? *None of your business, bud.* But the image of Juliana as his lover, straddling his thighs and arching to take his deep thrusts flashed in his mind. Heat oozed from his pores and his lungs stalled.

"Yeah. You got it," he croaked.

Keeping his distance from the bean counter was critical. She knew who he was, knew about his past. Worse, he feared she had the power to bring the self-centered SOB he used to be out of hiding. He couldn't allow that to happen.

When the man turned off the charm, he *really* turned it off. Juliana sighed. Rex hadn't given her a single sign of encouragement. And darn it, she didn't know how to flirt without looking like a bimbo with something in her eyes.

She reluctantly climbed from the mare's back. Was she so unattractive, so lacking in basic feminine charms that even a man who'd reportedly had women in every town his tour bus had rolled through wasn't interested? Ouch.

She had to find a way to get her plan back on track. In accounting, that meant understanding the parameters of the investigation, and the only way to achieve understanding was by asking questions, beginning with the nonthreatening ones and easing into the intrusive ones. She likened the practice to putting a jigsaw puzzle together, borders first.

"I don't suppose you'd consider selling Jelly Bean?" Not that she had much time to ride anymore, but this evening with a light breeze stirring her hair and the setting sun on her skin reminded her how much she missed having a horse in her life.

"She's not mine to sell. I bought the mare for Becky and Liza."

"And Becky and Liza are…?"

"My nieces."

"You bought them a horse? Did you also buy this property so they'd have somewhere to ride?"

He shook his head and his rope of shiny hair swished between his shoulder blades. The urge to tug the leather tie loose and see if the strands felt as thick and luxurious as they looked was totally out of character for her, but her neatly clipped-above-the-collar world hadn't allowed her to experience a man with longer hair without the width of a desk and the professional wall of her position at the bank between them. The men she'd dated in the past had all been the preppy, Ivy League type. Like Wally. Clean-cut. No rough edges.

Rex had rough edges aplenty.

"Farm's not mine. I rent the barn and a few acres from the owner. Her husband died last year. She leases the stable and the surrounding land to pay the mortgage."

"What made you choose to locate your business in Wilmington? We're not exactly horse country."

He flashed an irritated glance in her direction. Oops, had she sounded too much like a bank investigator? For a moment she thought he'd refuse to answer. "My brother-in-law is with Camp Lejeune's 4th Marine Expeditionary Brigade antiterrorism unit. I wanted to be nearby to help my sister with the girls when he's deployed. He's in Baghdad now."

Another chink in his bad-boy shell. What other discrepancies would she find if she looked past his rebel veneer? And did she really want to know? Her dislike of unanswered questions outweighed the need to keep her emotional distance. "You grew up on a ranch in tornado alley?"

"Yes," he barked in a mind-your-own-business voice and then took the reins from her and led the mare into the shade of the small four-stall barn.

Juliana's gaze immediately drifted to his firm behind in faded denim. When she realized what she was doing, she jerked her eyes back to the breadth of his shoulders. In the past, she'd been more concerned with a man's character instead of his looks, but she had to admit Rex had great packaging.

The smell of oats, hay and fresh shavings, and the hum of insects brought back memories. Until she'd turned seventeen, she'd spent almost as much time with her horse as her books, but when her old gelding had died of colic, she hadn't had the heart to replace him.

"Did you miss the ranch when you were touring?"

For several moments, Rex ignored her question while he exchanged the bridle for a halter and cross-tied the mare in the stall. He shoved his hand into the caddy carrying the brushes and stabbed a soft bristled-body brush in her direction. "Yes. Groom her."

Juliana couldn't imagine leaving Wilmington or Alden's

behind. For as far back as she could remember, she'd wanted to work in Alden's headquarters. The building's two-story foyer, with its marble pillars and the wrought-iron railings on the second-floor balcony, had been her own personal castle. She'd loved visiting after hours with her father, listening to the echo of their footsteps across the marble floor and the overwhelming silence of the place after the employees and customers had left for the day.

Because she'd wanted to stay near home and friends, she'd chosen to attend the local state university—much to her mother's dismay—rather than go to an Ivy League school out of state like so many of her classmates. The University of North Carolina at Wilmington had been her father's alma mater, and for once he'd spoken out against her mother's decrees and supported Juliana's decision to go to school locally and serve an internship at Alden's.

"Did you ever think of moving back?"

His gaze met hers over the horse's withers. The grooves beside his mouth deepened, drawing her attention to the dark evening beard shadowing his square jaw and upper lip. "You bought riding lessons not my life story."

Touchy, touchy. But she dealt with hostile people all the time. Digging into someone's accounts and revealing discrepancies didn't bring out the best in anyone. She'd learned to hold her ground and keep asking the questions until she had the information she needed. What exactly was she looking for here? She didn't know, but she'd keep digging until she found it.

"No, Rex, I didn't buy your biography, but if we're going to spend approximately sixteen hours together over the next four weeks, then we have to have something to discuss besides the weather. The story of my life would put us both to sleep, and since I imagine napping is frowned upon when riding or driving, I thought we'd try yours. You're welcome to volunteer other topics if you choose."

Scowling, he removed the mare's saddle and saddle pad, and deposited both on the top of the stall's wooden half door, and then braced his hands on either side of it. His shoulders, clad in another Renegade T-shirt, looked as stiff and broad as the beams supporting the barn roof.

"Yes, I missed the ranch. And I wish I'd gone back. But, I didn't. By the time I wised up, my sister had married and moved away and my parents were dead." He delivered the information in a matter-of-fact tone. His warning not to offer pity or sympathy came across loud and clear, but the ill-concealed pain in his voice brought a lump to Juliana's throat.

She ducked under the cross-tie, hesitated and then laid her hand on the rigid muscles of his back. "I'm sorry."

He flinched and stepped out of reach, then ducked to pick up the grooming caddy. Heat zinged through her from the brief contact, crackling and popping along her nerve endings in an unsettling manner. She lowered her arm and closed her prickling fingers into a fist. Before she could separate and label the avalanche of sensations, he straightened and turned. The emptiness in his eyes made her chest ache.

"Don't be. I got what I deserved. Groom the mare. I'll put the tack away and get her oats. We have to meet the reporter at Renegade in thirty minutes." He shoved the grooming box in her direction, snatched up the saddle and bridle as if they weighed nothing, and left.

Juliana stared after him. If Rex thought snarling like a wounded beast would put her off, then he'd miscalculated. The glimmer of softness he tried so hard to conceal had piqued her curiosity, and once Juliana had a puzzle to solve, she never gave up until she had every piece in place.

Three

"So tell me, Ms. Alden, why would the heiress to a banking empire need to buy a date?" Octavia Jenkins, the reporter, asked.

Heiress. Rex's chair wobbled precariously. He nearly fell over backward. Fighting for balance, he rocked forward. The front legs of the chair hit the floor with a thud. Up until now, he'd been completely relaxed. His half of the interview had gone well. He'd plugged the bar, served the reporter a selection of tasty appetizers and avoided discussing his aborted career.

"Your family *owns* the bank?" Rex asked. His first impression after the auction had been that Juliana had more money than sense, but he hadn't expected it to be *that* much money. Holy spit.

Juliana shifted in her seat and glanced around the restaurant as if checking to see who'd overheard his question. "I told you I worked for Alden Bank and Trust."

"You never told me your family *owned* it." And owned him,

or at least the note on his business. It would be her family's minions who would padlock Renegade's doors if Rex couldn't pay off the note. And he'd lose everything—his apartment and his business—since he'd invested all he had into Renegade. "You never told me your last name."

"You never asked."

He hadn't asked because he hadn't wanted to get involved beyond the lessons. So much for detachment.

The reporter looked up from her furious note-taking with a hungry glint in her eyes and a flush on her cocoa-colored skin. Rex had seen that look often enough in the past to know it meant trouble. "Were you trying to keep your family connections a secret?"

Juliana hesitated. "What would be the point? Every eligible male in the southeast knows who my family is."

And that, Rex deduced from Juliana's flat tone, was an issue. Had the banker's daughter experienced the degradation of being dated for what she represented rather than who she was as a person? He tamped down the empathy budding in his chest because he didn't want to have anything in common with Juliana. But she'd put a chink in the wall he'd worked so hard to build between them.

"Which leads us back to my original question, Ms. Alden. You should have men standing in line to wine and dine you. Why buy one?"

Juliana looked every inch the poised southern belle as she lifted her chin and smiled—a smile that Rex noted didn't reach her eyes—at the reporter. "My mother is the auction organizer. I wanted to support her efforts."

Bull. Rex didn't know how he knew it, but something in her voice and in her beauty-queen bearing told him that wasn't the real reason Juliana Alden, *banking heiress,* for crying out loud, had bought his package. His *auction* package—he clarified when a neglected part of his anatomy twitched to attention.

"And why did you choose Rex?"

Yeah, why him? He silently seconded Octavia's question. Lacing his fingers on the tabletop, he awaited Juliana's response.

"He's new in town and I've never ridden a motorcycle." More bull. He'd bet his Harley on it.

"You're playing welcoming committee?" He didn't bother to sugarcoat his disbelief.

"Is there something wrong with being neighborly?" She eyed him haughtily, but the tension in her features told its own tale. What was she hiding? Curiosity coiled in his gut.

Octavia persisted. "This had nothing to do with your recent thirtieth birthday, coming into your trust fund and your friends Andrea Montgomery and Holly Prescott also buying bachelors?"

Juliana paled and her eyes widened slightly. She inhaled a long breath and then slowly released it. Rex knew because the slow rise and fall of her breasts distracted him. He cursed the arousal strumming through his system, blinked and shifted his gaze back to her face.

"Only because each year Andrea, Holly and I do something to celebrate our birthdays. And yes, this year we each came into our trust funds, but since we all have well-paying careers, we don't really need the money. We decided to donate a portion of the money to a charitable cause, and the auction to support the disabled children's camp seemed as admirable a choice as any. Have you heard about the boat Dean Yachts has offered to design, build and donate to the cause?"

Octavia Jenkins waved the diversion aside. "I'll do a feature on that later. I want to talk about you." Leaning forward, she grinned mischievously and tilted her head conspiratorially toward Juliana. "You're a banker and he's a biker.

You can't get much more different than that. Taking a walk on the wild side never entered into your plans?"

Color rushed to Juliana's cheeks. She darted a panicked glance in Rex's direction, and then ducked her head and fussed with the silverware beside her plate. "No. That wasn't it at all."

Well, I'll be damned. If her guilty expression hadn't clued him in, then her rushed, breathless answer was a dead giveaway. The beautiful bean counter was lying through her perfect white teeth. And for some crazy reason, the prospect of Juliana getting wild *with him* turned him on like nobody's business.

Forget it, farm boy. Too risky.

"If you say so." Octavia closed her notebook and stood. "Well, that's all the questions I have tonight. I'll see you next week."

Rex rose. His mother had managed to drill some manners into his thick skull. He sat back down after the reporter had left and studied Juliana until she squirmed in her seat. She just didn't seem the type to rebel. And wasn't thirty a little old to get started on rebellion?

She bolted to her feet. "I should go, too."

Determined to get the truth out of her one way or another, Rex followed her outside, keeping pace beside her so he wouldn't be distracted by the sweet curve of her rear. The moon had yet to rise, but he could see well enough in the streetlights to know he was beginning to like the fit of her riding britches a little too much.

"Why did you buy my package?" he asked as they neared her car.

She turned on the cobblestone sidewalk. "I told you."

"You're off the record now. No reporter in sight. Let's have the truth, Juliana. Why me?"

Her face flushed with more than indignation. She shifted uneasily. "I beg your pardon? Are you calling me a liar?"

"Admit it. You fed that reporter a load of manure."

If she stood any straighter, her spine would snap. "Mr. Tanner—"

"Rex," he corrected and moved closer. Without the killer heels, the top of her head barely reached his chin.

She retreated, bumping into the lamppost behind her. Milky light streamed over her, painting ribbons of silver in her dark hair. A soft breeze ruffled the strands around her face. She tipped her head back and her lips parted on a shaky breath, and her pink tongue slipped out to wet them.

"*Rex*, then. Why would you suspect I had an ulterior motive for bidding on you?" Her damp lips and breathless tone hit him like the business end of a cattle prod, sending a jolt of electricity through him.

"You turned ten shades of red when the reporter asked if you wanted to take a walk on the wild side. Looked guilty as hell to me."

Her lashes fluttered and her gaze fell. "I did not."

"Did too." He'd learned from experience that the only way to deal with a problem was to confront it. Running didn't work. Ignoring it wouldn't either. He propped one arm on the post above her head and leaned in until only inches separated their faces. "Wanting to see if Nashville's bad boy can live up to his hell-raising reputation?"

"Of course not," she said too quickly. But her gaze shifted to his mouth and her breath puffed against his chin in shallow bursts. The tight points of her breasts pushed at her blouse.

She wanted him, and damned if the feeling wasn't mutual. He swallowed the sudden flood of moisture in his mouth and cursed the unwelcome response drumrolling through his veins. Kissing the bank owner's daughter would be a big mistake, but part of him wanted to forget common sense, taste her red lips and feel her slender length against him.

Go for it, his awakening libido urged. Then maybe the simmering sexual awareness between them would die a natural death and they could get on with the lessons. She wasn't his type and he sure wasn't hers.

He cupped her jaw with his right hand. The warm velvety texture of her skin surprised him. Tempted him. His fingertips teased her earlobe, her nape, and then closed around the cool satin of her hair. He tugged, tilting back her head and lifting her lips closer to his.

"Is this what you want, Juliana?" He cupped her jodhpur-covered bottom, pulling her closer, and lowered his head. In his hypersensitive state, her swiftly indrawn breath sounded as loud as a jet engine. Her fingers spread over his belly and dug into his waist, starting a fire he wasn't sure he could put out. But she didn't push him away. Her lashes drifted down and his lids grew heavy in response. His mouth hovered above hers, close enough that he could taste her sweet breath, and then sanity slapped him upside the head.

What in the hell are you doing, Tanner?

He hesitated, examining her flushed face, parted lips and the dark fan of her long lashes against her cheeks. Damn. The reporter had nailed Juliana's motive. The banking heiress was using him. And if he gave in to the urge to kiss her—hell, the urge to take her right here against the lamppost—he'd be using her, too.

Been there. Done that. Not going back.

He didn't want to be that selfish bastard again, and risking any kind of involvement with a woman whose family could pull the rug out from under his business could be career suicide. Because when the relationship ended—and it would end—there'd be hell to pay.

Swallowing a sobering lungful of air, he battled the need twisting through him like a tornado and shoved himself away. A sexy protest emerged from Juliana's mouth, but he ignored it.

"If a walk on the wild side is what you're after, Ms. Alden, find another sucker." Turning on his heel, he left temptation—and certain disaster—behind.

Thursday evening arrived long before Juliana could get a handle on her reaction to the near-miss kiss and the sting of Rex's rejection. But she wouldn't let a little discomfiture derail her agenda.

"Plan B. If the mountain won't come to Mohammed," she muttered as she turned her car into the stable's driveway.

Over the past two and a half days, she'd launched a full-scale fact-finding mission. By her calculations, she was as prepared for today's lesson as she possibly could be. She'd memorized the magazines recommended by her twenty- and thirty-something coworkers, bought clothing deemed appropriate by said magazines for casual dates with a hot guy and learned everything between the covers of the Department of Motor Vehicles booklet Rex had given her. To top it off, on her lunch hour yesterday she'd visited the local motorcycle dealership. The salesman had fitted her with the proper safety gear to the tune of several hundred dollars, and she'd spent a good part of last night curled up with a book—the Harley owner's manual.

She spotted Rex standing beside his motorcycle. The bees in her stomach buzzed into flight. Once again, he wore jeans and a Renegade T-shirt. His closed countenance brought heat to her cheeks. He hadn't forgotten their last encounter or her panting eagerness. Neither had she.

If he could disturb her that much without actually kissing her, then what kind of havoc could he wreak if—*when*—their lips connected? She trembled in her new biker boots at the possibility of exploring further.

She'd never had sex just for the sex's sake and wasn't totally comfortable with the idea now. In the past, each relationship she'd allowed to progress into intimacy had been one that she'd thought might eventually lead to love and marriage. None had, and she readily admitted that was mostly her fault. She'd never been head-over-heels in love or anywhere close to lust and that made it all too easy to get caught up in her job and forget her boyfriends. The guys eventually got tired of being neglected and dumped her.

Forget past failures. Focus on future successes. Wrapping herself in the knowledge that she looked young, hip and available, she took a deep breath for courage, parked and climbed from the car.

Come and get me, bad boy.

Rex's gaze lasered in on her clothing as she closed the distance between them, and he snapped to attention like a military man. His darkening expression looked more ominous than the storm clouds on the distant horizon.

Hold your ground. Don't let him rattle you.

"Good evening, Rex." Juliana's manufactured smile wobbled on her lips when he didn't return it. She extricated the hard rectangle of her motorcycle learner's permit from the pocket of her snug new jeans and handed it to him. "I'm ready for my driving lesson."

He took the permit, but his eyes examined her, not the card. She struggled with the urge to hitch up the low-riding stretch jeans and cross her arms over her close-fitting camisole top with its built-in push-up bra. At the moment, Juliana would have welcomed anything that would cover the two-inch wide band of bare skin around her midsection. Even the navel ring the sales clerk had tried but failed to talk her into sounded good since it would have covered part of her navel. These clothes were so not her, although she had to acknowledge the heady surge of power caused by Rex's widening pupils and devouring glance.

Rex blinked, handed back the license and abruptly pivoted toward the bike. "We'll start with ground work."

His voice sounded deeper than she remembered, but the stiff set of his shoulders looked familiar. How did he turn the charm on and off so easily? At the auction and with the reporter, he'd been Mr. Too-Hot-To-Handle, but with her, he was Mr. Don't-Mess-With-Me. Which was the real Rex Tanner and what was he thinking behind that blank expression?

Juliana wiggled her license back into her pocket and reached deep for the bravado to get through the next two hours. "I borrowed a manual and a video from the Harley dealership. I can name most of the parts of a motorcycle."

He grunted a nonanswer while he polished a spot off the fuel tank with the hem of his shirt. A glimpse of flat abdomen dusted with dark curls sucked the breath from her lungs.

Her studiousness obviously hadn't impressed him. But that was no surprise. She'd never met a guy who liked brainy women. She ought to know. She'd run off more than her share. *Take the initiative.* She cleared her throat. "Can I drive your motorcycle today?"

He shot her a hard look. "My bike is too heavy for a beginner to ride alone, and you're not wearing the proper gear."

"I wasn't wearing the proper gear Saturday night, either. I have a leather jacket and gloves in my car, if you insist, but it's a little hot for those, isn't it? Couldn't you ride behind me and help me keep the Harley upright?"

A muscle in the corner of Rex's jaw bunched. "Show me what you know."

Her heart *kaboomed* in her chest. *You can handle this.*

You're used to proving yourself, and you give presentations at work all the time. Her mental pep talk didn't keep her palms from dampening or her lungs from constricting. "Okay."

Juliana tried to block Rex's presence behind her from her mind as she circled the bike, naming the parts and regurgitating most of the salesman's spiel. She was out of breath by the time she finished and faced Rex again.

Was that a spark of approval lurking in his narrowed eyes? "That was today's lesson. Next week's, too. Did you memorize the entire manual?"

Her cheeks burned. She grimaced and hugged her waist. So data was her thing. Big deal. "Pretty much."

He smoothed a hand over his tied-back hair. Juliana curled her fingers against the need to test its texture. What was wrong with her? She'd never had the urge to stroke a man's hair before Rex, but she yearned to know if his was thick and springy or soft and silky. It was definitely well cared for, with bluntly trimmed ends and glossy sheen.

He exhaled long and slow. She caught a whiff of mint on his breath. "Put on the helmet and climb on."

The bottom dropped out of her stomach, and then she scrambled to do as he instructed before he changed his mind or she chickened out. Both very real possibilities. Her legs quivered as she mounted the bike, and her hands trembled when she reached for the rubber grips on the handlebars. The Harley felt bigger, broader than last time, but last time she'd been on the back and not in the driver's seat.

Rex donned his own helmet. He looked so sexy and rebellious dressed all in black from his boots to his helmet that her heart went wild. And then he climbed on behind her. Their bodies didn't touch, but his heat spanned the gap between them, and the fine hairs on her body rose as if magnetized toward him. His shoulders bracketed hers as his thickly muscled arms reached around her, and his hands flanked hers on the handgrips.

Juliana swallowed to relieve the sudden dryness of her mouth. Her pulse roared in her ears, nearly deafening her to his low-pitched instructions.

"When we're ready to roll, I want you to park your feet on top of my boots to get a feel for how I shift the gears. I'll cover your hands with mine to work the throttle and brakes." He suited words to action. His palms were hot and slightly rough against her skin. His fingers wove between hers.

Who knew the sides of her fingers could be so receptive?

Rex continued to rattle off safety tips and general info. Juliana struggled to focus on his words, but fear and an alien sensation intertwined low in her belly, interfering with her ability to process the instructions in a coherent manner. Good thing she'd picked up most of the info from the manual and driver's safety book.

"I'm going to start the engine, and then we'll take a slow lap around the farm."

She started trembling before the motor rumbled to life.

"Relax," he called over the motor's throaty growl.

Easier said than done. She wasn't sure which intimidated her more—the man behind her or the mechanical beast beneath her. The man, she decided, but by a narrow margin.

Rex rolled the bike forward to disengage the kickstand. His chest nudged her back and his breath teased the hair at the base of her neck beneath the round, bowl-shaped helmet. The insides of his thick biceps brushed the outsides of her arms and she shivered. This time there was no mistaking the cause. Sexual awareness. Good to know she wasn't incapable. She hoped the engine vibration concealed her response from Rex or she'd be in for another brush-off. Later, when she wasn't on the back of this monster, she'd scrutinize the budding sensations and the fact that she had erogenous zones in the oddest locations. That she had functioning erogenous zones at all was newsworthy in itself.

"Squeeze the clutch and put the bike in gear." His left hand manipulated hers over the mechanism on the handlebar and his left foot shifted the gears beneath hers. "And then you case the clutch back out again," he said over her shoulder. "Slow and steady."

The bike sprang forward, thumping Juliana into Rex's chest. Her breaths shortened—not from fear of the bike, but because of the man curved against her spine. His warmth encircled her and her scanty camisole wasn't much of a barrier. She considered reestablishing the space between them, but the urge to stay burrowed against his chest was too strong to fight.

"Shift into second." His foot and hands moved and the bike picked up speed on the long gravel driveway. The power of the engine pulsated through her and each bump in the road chafed her body against Rex's like an all-over massage.

Hello! You can't learn two dangerous skills at once. Concentrate on learning to ride the motorcycle first or you'll get yourself killed. There will be time to work on the man-woman thing with Rex later.

Maintaining her focus wasn't as easy as it should have been, but Juliana concentrated on the changing engine sounds and tried to block out the rise and fall of Rex's chest against her shoulder blades.

Rex kept the bike on a steady course over the flat farm road for one lap around the property and then another and another. By the third circuit Juliana could anticipate when it was time to change gears and brace herself for the slide of Rex's thigh against hers before it happened. Her tense muscles slowly relaxed, allowing other sensations to penetrate the sensual haze fogging her brain.

The setting sun kissed her cheeks, and the sweet scent of honeysuckle filled her lungs. Warm, humid air caressed her arms and the narrow strip of bare skin at her waist.

I could get used to this. I could even like it.

Juliana Alden, biker chick. Her mother would have a stroke. A chuckle slipped from Juliana's lips, and then she sobered and said a prayer of thanks that her mother had decided to punish her with the silent treatment since the auction. She hadn't caught grief from her other family members, either, because her father had been out of town and her brother had been occupied with Holly.

Ick. Not a path she wanted to travel.

Rex downshifted and pulled the Harley to a stop. "Your turn."

Juliana's pulse, which had slowed to a steady thump over the last fifteen minutes, galloped once more. She twisted on the seat. Rex's face was so close she could see every pore, every individual blade of beard stubble, and each tiny crease at the corners of his eyes and on the surface of his lips. *Gulp.* "Already?"

She lifted her gaze to his. For several seconds, he didn't look away and then his dark chocolate eyes lowered to her mouth. Her breath lodged in her chest. She inhaled unsteadily. All she had to do was lean forward and—

Rex released the handlebars, slid back on the seat and fisted his hands on his thighs.

"You're ready to drive." His voice sounded an octave lower than usual. Rough. Rusty. *Sexy.*

Juliana wet her parched lips and batted down her disappointment. If she'd ever wanted a man to kiss her this badly, she couldn't remember the occasion. She'd certainly never experienced even a fraction of this much need for Wally.

Wally, she mentally cringed and faced forward again. How could she have forgotten about him? He was *nice* and steady and her parents liked him. According to her mother, his administrative assistant, a divorcée with three children, had bought him at the auction. How could Donna afford a bachelor at the obscene prices they'd brought Saturday night? A fifty-pound bag of guilt dropped on Juliana's shoulders. Wally had probably footed the bill. Had he been expecting Juliana to buy him? If so, she owed him an apology.

Perhaps by the end of the month marrying Wally wouldn't seem like selling out her dream of finding true desire. If she wasn't capable of heart-racing passion, then why hold out for it?

A cloud passed over the sun and she shivered. The rebel behind her would never understand the allure of a risk-free option or Juliana's fear that safe, sensible Wally might be the best she could do. "Are you sure I can handle the motorcycle?"

"Yeah. I'll be right here behind you if you need help." He kicked out the passenger foot pegs.

Juliana's palms dampened on the rubber grips. She missed the reassuring warmth of Rex against her back and the protective embrace of his arms and legs bracketing hers. She tested the clutch and throttle, and then lifted her foot to the gear pedal.

Rex's hands settled on her waist. The unexpected contact against her bare skin sent a shock wave through her. She released the clutch too quickly, and the bike jerked forward and choked off, slamming him against her back.

"Easy. Try again." His breath teased her ear.

How could she concentrate with his hands scorching her? As if he'd read her thoughts, he shifted them upward, away from her bare skin, but bringing them to rest on her rib cage just below her breasts. Not an improvement if clear thought was the goal. The thin fabric of her camisole did nothing to block the transfer of heat between his skin and hers.

Grinding her molars against the surprising need to cover his palms and slide them up a few inches, she put the bike back in neutral, fired the engine and tried again. The machine lurched and cut off. Her third and fourth tries weren't any more successful. Each hop smacked her against Rex, increasing her tension and frustration. "I can't do this."

"You can." His no-nonsense tone cut through her embarrassment. "Would it help if I put my hands back on the handlebars?"

"Yes." Heat rushed to her cheeks and steamed her scalp inside the helmet. She didn't dare turn to look at his face. "I'm having a bit of trouble concentrating when you…touch me."

His whistled breath sounded loud in the sudden silence.

"Drive." It sounded as if he'd forced the word through clenched teeth. His hands bracketed hers beside the controls.

Closing her eyes, Juliana tried to gather her scattered wits and visualized the required steps. The bike rolled forward. She quickly lifted her lids and fought to stay away from the white board fences. Changing into second gear went smoother. She wanted to pump her arms in triumph, but didn't dare release her stranglehold on the grips.

She'd just shifted into third gear when Rex moved his hands back to her waist. Each of his fingers sent a marching band of awareness parading across her skin. Her jaws clamped on a whimper. It took one hundred percent of her attention to keep from wrecking the motorcycle into a nearby apple tree.

And then it hit her. She was driving Rex's big, bad, black Harley. Sure, Rex was behind her, but *she* was in control of the machine. Adrenaline surged through her. She lifted her face to the wind and laughed out loud.

Her joy lasted all of five minutes. A fat raindrop landed on her cheek. Moments later the bottom fell out of the clouds and rain poured. Rex leaned forward and yelled in her ear. "Head for the barn. Park inside."

Juliana steered the motorcycle toward shelter and opened the throttle as much as she dared. She raced through raindrops pelting her arms and face like bee stings. Within seconds her clothing was saturated and goose bumps covered her skin. She downshifted and pulled through the open barn doors.

Rex reached around her to kill the engine, and then lowered the kickstand and climbed from the bike. Still high on her accomplishment, Juliana followed. She tugged off her helmet and set it beside Rex's on the seat. The rain hammered on the metal roof with deafening force, but the storm couldn't dampen her excitement, and she couldn't keep the grin off her face.

She—boring account auditor Juliana Alden—had driven a motorcycle and not just any motorcycle, but a *hog*…the most notorious machine on the road. If she could control this monster, then she could control anything—even her recently unsettled life.

She wanted to shout with joy, to laugh out loud and to celebrate her accomplishment. Instead, she threw her arms around Rex's neck and planted a kiss on his bristly cheek. "Thank you. Thank you. Thank you."

His hands fastened on her bare waist with scalding heat, but instead of pushing her away, Rex held her captive. His warmth penetrated her cold, saturated clothing, raising her temperature inside and out. Her breasts prodded his chest and his thighs laced with hers. Aroused male, encased in steaming wet denim, pressed against her belly. She shivered, but not from cold.

Juliana tilted her head back and met his gaze in the shadowy barn. Coffee-colored eyes burned into hers before tracing the rain trails across her face. A lone drop quivered on the corner of her lip. He bent and sipped up the droplet.

She gasped at the lightning force of the tiny caress and her heart slammed against her ribs. Her fingers curled into his shoulders, and then Rex's mouth took hers in a devouring kiss.

Hard. Urgent. His tongue tangled with hers and his hands splayed over her buttocks, yanking her closer. A dam burst. Shock receded and pleasure flooded Juliana's bloodstream.

She cradled his bristly cheeks and held on as unfamiliar but delicious sensations danced through her. His face and lips were damp from the rain, but hot, oh so hot. His evening beard abraded her palms and then her fingers reached his hair. She tugged the strip of leather free and twined the soft, springy strands around her fingers. The ends were damp and cool from the rain, a complete contrast to the fire flickering to life inside her.

His hands raked upward from her hips to her ribs. Her nipples tightened and her breath hitched in anticipation. One big hand cupped her breast and her knees quaked.

He stroked her tight nipple, stirring a swarm of need low in her belly. She'd never experienced anything so intense, so incredibly urgent. His hard thigh pressed the juncture of her thighs and Juliana shamelessly pushed back. Sparks ignited in her veins and a whimper of pleasure climbed her throat.

Rex jerked his head back, swore and set her away. He stalked across the barn to stare out the open door at the rain blowing almost horizontally. Wind whipped strands of his hair away from his rigid jaw.

Confused, Juliana blinked. Why had he stopped? Surely after that kiss, he had to know she was interested?

Maybe you're a lousy kisser. It's not as if you get much practice.

Her cheeks stung with a combination of embarrassment and beard burn, but her skin still prickled with need. Slowly, the rattle of the rain on the roof and the boom of thunder drowned out the roar of her pulse in her ears. Warmth seeped out of her wet clothing, leaving her chilled to the bone.

Examine the facts.

Rex Tanner wanted her. She'd seen the hunger in his deep, dark eyes, felt it in his kiss and in the brand of his tight-fitting jeans against her belly. But he wasn't happy about his desire. Why?

According to her online research, he'd been with dozens of other women. Juliana touched her lips. Was there something wrong with her? Some intrinsically feminine component she lacked?

Maybe he didn't like being with a woman who'd bought him any more than she liked the idea of buying a date.

Putting the embarrassment over the circumstances of their meeting aside, Juliana reveled in her discovery. For the first time in her life, she'd tasted the mind-melting passion other women whispered about. And if she wasn't completely incapable of desire, then what did that mean for her future with Wally?

She didn't have the answer, but one thing was certain. Her appetite for breaking the rules that had governed her life to this point had been whetted, and she couldn't wait until her next lesson.

Four

Could the day get any worse?

In answer to Rex's question, the rain switched over to hail. It struck the metal roof like drumsticks on a snare drum.

So much for the weather forecaster's twenty percent chance of scattered showers.

To get away from the temptation of the woman behind him, Rex considered stepping into the storm and letting the ice pelt his thick, horny hide, but he didn't have any dry clothes and he'd ridden over on his Harley. The temperature had dropped by at least twenty degrees in the past ten minutes. He'd be hypothermic before he could get home.

Lightning sliced the sky and thunder shook the ground. A frigid wind whipped through the open door, cooling his overheated skin and blowing his hair across his eyes. What had Juliana done with his leather string? He turned to ask but the question died on his lips.

Juliana hugged herself. Her teeth chattered and goose bumps covered her bare arms, shoulders and even the tantalizing strip of paler skin across her belly. His protective instincts kicked in. "Let me see if I can find something to cover your head, and we'll get you to your car."

"I'm n-not driv-ving in th-that."

He could barely hear her over the hail. "Your car has a heater."

"It's not worth g-getting hit by lightning to g-get to it."

Good point. She'd parked a hundred yards away across an open area. The afternoon heat had already escaped the building, but he rolled the barn door closed anyway. He had to get Juliana warm. All he had to offer was his damp T-shirt. That wouldn't help.

"C'mon." He led her into the tack room and shut the door. The temperature inside the eight-foot-square windowless room was marginally warmer. He searched the dim space hoping he'd somehow overlooked something in his cleaning binge that Juliana could wrap up in, but he found nothing. The barn had been a disaster when he'd leased it. Rats had taken over and made bedding out of any available material, so he'd scoured the place from corner to corner and thrown out everything. All that remained were a metal tack trunk, a steel drum for the feed and a rough cedar bench.

"Here." Dusky pink swept her cheekbones as she offered his strip of braided leather.

He tied his hair and tried to ignore her chattering teeth, but couldn't. His control dangled from a fraying rope and after that kiss the last thing he needed to do was touch her. Just his luck that his libido would emerge after months of hibernation for a woman he ought to avoid at all cost.

The fact that she was freezing her tail off without complaint got to him. Her silent shivers got to him. Even her damp flowers-and-spice scent got to him. In fact, everything about Juliana Alden knocked him sideways. "Turn around."

Eyes narrowing, she hesitated and then turned her back. He brushed her hands out of the way and briskly chafed the cool skin of her upper arms. Her quick gasp tugged his groin. The firmness of the muscles beneath his hands surprised him. He'd expected a desk jockey to be soft, but Juliana obviously kept in shape from her tight arms to her tight a—

Don't go there.

"I thought the weather back home was crazy." Home. Except for his parents' funeral, Rex hadn't been back to the ranch since the day he'd turned eighteen, and even though the property had been sold, he still thought of the ranch as home. But his place was here now. Near Kelly, Mike and the girls.

Juliana tilted her head and looked at him over her shoulder. Her hair glided over his fingers in a soft-as-silk caress. "The storm front sitting off the coast must have backed into the cold front coming from the northwest. Wilmington gets weird weather when that happens. In the winter, we get snow, which—trust me—is odd for the North Carolina coast."

Her shivers slowed then ceased. Her skin warmed and her muscles relaxed beneath his hands, but he didn't want to let her go. A jolt of pure hunger hit him low and hard. It had been too damned long since he'd stroked a woman's smooth, supple skin. Juliana leaned into him, and the desire to wrap his arms around her, bury his face against her neck and cradle her breasts in his palms grabbed him in a stranglehold.

He dropped his hands and stepped away, but there was nowhere to run in the confined space. Saddle racks jutted from the walls, forcing him to stand only inches from temptation. "We'll stay here until the hail stops and then you need to go home."

She faced him. "What about you?"

"I came on my bike. I'll wait until the rain lets up."

"And if it doesn't, you'll spend the night? Where? Here?" She gestured to the narrow four-foot bench.

"If I have to. I've slept on worse."

A stubborn glint entered her blue eyes and her chin lifted. The single, bare lightbulb revealed a reddened patch of beard burn along her jaw. Damn. He hadn't realized he'd been so rough. "I'm not leaving you here."

His pulse misfired. "There's no point in both of us being cold and uncomfortable."

"That's exactly why you'll be reasonable and accept my offer of a ride home. I have a jacket in the car, so once the hail and lightning stop and I can get to it, *I* won't be cold." Her gaze dropped to the points of his nipples clearly outlined by his damp, clingy T-shirt. "And I keep a quilt in my trunk. You can use that."

His reaction wasn't caused by cold, but he wouldn't correct her. If she looked lower, she'd figure it out by herself.

She tapped a finger to her swollen lips, and just like that, the memory of the kiss reignited the fire in his blood. Soft lips. Satiny tongue. He clamped his teeth, fisted his hands and fought to extinguish the blaze.

"Are you worried that someone will steal your motorcycle if you leave it here overnight?"

He should lie and say yes. It beat the hell out of admitting that he needed to put some distance between them before he pulled her back into his arms and put the strength of the bench behind her to the test. The flimsy thing probably wouldn't hold their combined weight.

Not something you need to be thinking about, bucko.

"No. The owner has a couple of dogs she lets loose after dark. They keep an eye on things."

"Then I'll give you a ride."

"There's no need—"

"I guess you could call for a pizza delivery and hitch a ride back with the driver if you're afraid to ride with me."

Afraid? He straightened at the insult to his pride. "I don't have a cell phone."

He'd given it up along with most of the other trappings of success. Besides, he didn't want his Nashville associates tracking him down. Not that he was hiding. He hadn't done anything illegal. But he had lost all respect for the man he'd become, so he'd cut those ties. Permanently.

"Mine's in the car. You can use it—if you insist on being impractical."

That set his teeth on edge. "I need to see to Jelly Bean. If the rain hasn't stopped by the time I finish then I'll take that ride."

He let himself out of the tack room and headed for the mare's stall. He hadn't prayed this hard for the weather to change since his first headlining concert in an outdoor venue. Twenty thousand fans had come to see him in the pouring rain. And they'd stayed despite the weather. He'd done his damnedest not to let them down, and from here on he'd do his best not to let himself down by crossing the line into temptation. But there were no guarantees of success. Juliana Alden had a way of getting around his common sense.

He had to get out of this auction package. He couldn't afford to repay her the thousands she'd bid on him, since most of his cash was tied up in Renegade, but he could afford the four hundred the local dealership charged for the motorcycle driver-safety course. And the farm owner used to ride the horse-show circuit. He'd bet he could talk her into giving Juliana riding lessons in exchange for him doing a few more chores around here.

Yeah, that's it. Juliana would get her lessons—just not from him. As soon as he got her back to Renegade, he'd tell her goodbye.

* * *

"Let me buy you a drink."

Juliana's heart missed a beat at Rex's low-voiced invitation. She searched his face, but the streetlights didn't penetrate the shadowy interior of her car. Had she misread his stony silence during the drive back?

Her palms dampened and anticipation danced along her spine. Would he invite her upstairs? She wanted to be corrupted out of her Goody Two-shoes image. Really, she did, and she had a brand new box of condoms in her purse to prove it, but frankly, the idea of getting naked with Rex gave her heart palpitations, because she was starting to like him a little too much for this to be a wham-bam-thank-you-ma'am kind of encounter.

Last chance.

"Um…sure. I'd love a drink."

He circled the car, took the umbrella from her and guided her toward Renegade without touching her, but Juliana was highly conscious of his hand hovering at the small of her back.

The bartender looked up as soon as they entered. "Your sister's upstairs and, man, she's a mess."

"Give me a minute," Rex called to Juliana. He yanked open the door to his apartment and took the steps two at a time. Juliana eyed the crowd of construction workers leering at her from the bar. Unwilling to deal with the kind of attention her skimpy attire drew, she followed Rex upstairs.

As she entered his apartment, Juliana noted the suitcase beside the door and then the woman sobbing in Rex's arms. Unsure if she was intruding, Juliana hesitated.

"What's up, Kel?"

The petite brunette drew back. Her face was blotchy and red from crying. Fresh tears streamed from her dark eyes as she drew a ragged breath. "Mike's been hurt. He's in critical condition in Landstuhl, Germany."

"The military hospital?" Rex asked.

"Yes. He might—" Her voice broke. "They said he might not make it."

He gripped her shoulders. "What do you need me to do? Name it. I'll do it."

His tender tone vibrated through Juliana. What would it be like to have a man care that much?

"I need you to keep the girls."

"Whoa." He recoiled and then dragged a hand over his jaw. "Where are Becky and Liza now?"

"Asleep." She pointed toward a closed door. "I can't take them with me, Rex. I know you have to work, but I have to go. I *have* to see Mike."

"Yeah, you do, but Kelly, I'm not set up to watch the girls for more than a few hours. What about one of the other military wives?"

"You know I don't know them well enough to ask. Please, Rex. I don't have anybody else. And I have to get there be-fore…before…" A sob choked off her words.

The furrow between Rex's eyebrows deepened. Frustration and a touch of panic rolled off him in waves. "I can't close Renegade. I'm barely—" His gaze flashed to Juliana and then back to his sister. "I can't afford to close my doors and I don't have the staff to cover for me. The girls can't stay downstairs, and I can't leave them up here alone. I want to help, but I don't know how I can."

Juliana's heart squeezed in sympathy. The woman's hus-band was critically injured and thousands of miles away. If the situation was as grave as Kelly said, then there wasn't time to research alternative child care. Besides, from what Juliana's coworkers had said, good child-care centers had waiting lists.

And then the answer fell into place—an answer that could solve several problems at once. Irma, the lady who'd been more like a mother than a nanny to Juliana, had become increasingly lonely and unhappy since having to retire. Juliana worried about her. Helping Kelly meant helping Irma and there wasn't anything Juliana wouldn't do for Irma. And, Juliana admitted, she wouldn't mind having the opportunity to spend more time with Rex and uncover yet another layer of the complex man she'd bought.

"Perhaps I could help."

Both heads swiveled toward her.

"No," Rex barked.

"Who are you?" his sister asked simultaneously.

"I'm Juliana Alden. Rex's...friend. My evenings and weekends are free, and I suspect the lady who used to be my nanny would love to keep the girls for a few hours a day when either Rex or I can't be with them."

Hope flared in the eyes the same dark coffee shade as Rex's. "You like kids?"

"Yes, although I confess I don't have loads of experience. But I'm a fast learner and I don't give up easily."

"If you could cover the girls in the evenings then Rex could watch them in the mornings, and your nanny could cover midday."

Rex stepped between them. "We don't need to bother Juliana. I'll work something out. I'll call an employment agency or a local day care—"

Kelly looked horrified. "The girls are upset enough. They don't need that kind of upheaval."

"My town-house complex has a pool and a playground," Juliana added, earning a glare from Rex. "Irma could watch them at my place, and I grew up in Wilmington, so I know where all the parks and yummy ice-cream shops are located. How long do you think you'll be gone?"

Kelly gestured toward the suitcase. "I packed enough clothing for the girls for a week, but I don't know. It all depends on M-Mike."

"We don't want to inconvenience you." Rex didn't say *back off*, but it came through loud and clear in his clipped words.

Juliana ignored him. "It's no trouble at all. In fact, I'm sure Irma would love to have something to keep her occupied. She's recently retired and not enjoying it."

Kelly threw her arms around Juliana. "Thank you so much. I'm so worried about Mike. What if he—" Her voice cracked and a fresh wave of sobs racked her.

"I'm sure he's getting the best care possible." Juliana put an arm around Kelly's shoulder. "When does your flight leave?"

"Midnight."

Juliana glanced at her watch. "It's almost nine now. We need to get you to the airport. I'll drive you. Rex can stay here with the girls." She turned to Rex. "I'll be back as soon as I get Kelly checked in, and we'll work out the details."

Juliana's last glimpse of Rex as she led his sister out the door wasn't reassuring. His scowl and fisted hands didn't bode well for their week together.

Gentle, loving brother. Doting uncle. Rebel. And too proud to accept her assistance. The man's contradictions intrigued her more than a falsified account, and Juliana couldn't wait to figure him out.

Who'd have suspected the bean counter would be so difficult to shake loose?

Rex had invited Juliana in to buy her a drink and dump her, and here she was back in his apartment long after midnight. Worse, it looked as though he'd be stuck with her until Kelly returned. It wouldn't be a hardship if his body didn't hum like a generator when she was around, but that was one engine he couldn't afford to start.

What really pissed him off was that as much as he resented her help, he really didn't have a choice since he couldn't come up with another solution. Damn his sister for refusing to become a part of the support network on base. But Kelly had always been an ostrich who preferred ignoring a problem instead of dealing with it. She couldn't handle the tragedies of other husbands being killed in action, so she isolated herself from the wives and turned a blind eye to the possibility instead of preparing for it.

Reluctantly, he settled beside Juliana on the sofa. She looked slightly rumpled and incredibly sexy. With her lids at half-mast, she looked tired enough to nod off at any second. The urge to pull her head onto his shoulder wasn't a welcome one.

She covered a yawn with her hand. "I called Irma on the way to the airport and set everything up. She's thrilled about watching the girls, and Kelly's relieved that they'll be in experienced hands most of the time.

"Kelly, Irma and I worked out a schedule. The girls will spend the nights here with you. You'll deal with mornings and then drop them off at my town house. On weekdays, Irma will take over until I get home in the evenings. Becky and Liza will have dinner with me, and then I'll bring them back here for baths and bedtime. I'll stay until you can take over, and I'll watch them on the weekends."

Juliana had made plans, but she'd missed a few critical details. "Hold it. Most nights I don't get upstairs before two. That's too late for you to drive home, and I only have two bedrooms—the girls' and mine."

She sat up straighter. "Bedrooms aren't an issue because I'm leaving each night as soon as you get home." She rose, picked up her purse and took a step toward the door. "I'd like to stop by in the morning on my way to work so the girls can meet me. I think that would make them more comfortable with me tomorrow evening."

For a lady who was supposedly good with numbers, she wasn't adding them up very well. He rose and parked his hands on his hips. "How far do you live from here?"

"About twenty or thirty minutes, depending on traffic."

"And what time do you usually get up in the morning?"

"Six, but I'll rise earlier to come here."

"If you drive home, you'll get about three hours sleep before you have to get up and come back." As much as Rex hated to admit it, there was only one solution. "Starting tonight, you'll have to sleep here."

Juliana's mouth dropped open. She quickly snapped it shut again and backed toward the door. "That's not necessary."

"No way around it unless you can live without sleep. It's late. You're exhausted. Take my bed. The sheets are clean. I'll sleep on the sofa."

Her eyes rounded. "But I don't have clothes or…anything."

The idea of Juliana sliding naked between his sheets guaranteed he'd have a hard time sleeping—hard being the operative word. "I'll loan you a T-shirt. We can throw what you're wearing into the washer. We'll get the girls ready together in the morning, and then you can go home to dress for work. I'll follow you. You can show us around and introduce us to Irma."

A hand fluttered to her throat. Several silent seconds ticked past while she digested the new plan. "I…okay. But we could um…share the bed?"

Flames licked through his veins, singeing the edges of his common sense. He knew he shouldn't—*couldn't*—have her, but that didn't mean he'd be able to control himself if he had to lie beside her all night. "And then neither of us would sleep."

Her skin flushed and her lips parted on a ragged breath. "I'm sure we could figure something out."

Need throbbed insistently in his gut. "No."

He stalked past her, retrieved the largest T-shirt he owned—the more she covered the better—a new toothbrush and a bath towel. "Soap, shampoo, toothpaste are all in the bathroom. If you need anything else just yell."

After a moment's hesitation, she accepted the small stack. "Thank you."

He hesitated, but then forced himself to say what he had to. "No, thank you, Juliana. I didn't have a backup plan, and Kelly knew it. If you hadn't stepped in, I'm not sure what would have happened. I owe you."

And he wished like hell he didn't because those kinds of debts always came back to bite you.

Rex had been in the room while she'd slept.

Juliana raked her hair out of her face and stared at the neatly stacked pile of folded clothing—her panties on top—sitting on the edge of the dresser beside her purse. Her heart thumped out an irregular rhythm.

She shoved back the covers on the big leather platform bed and rose. Ten minutes later, after showering and dressing, she followed the smell of freshly-brewed coffee to the kitchen and stopped in her tracks.

Rex, wearing only jeans riding low on his hips, leaned against the counter clutching a mug and staring into it like it held the elixir of life. His hair was loose and rumpled, and beard stubble shadowed his jaw and upper lip. Long hair should lessen his manly impact, but if anything the soft strands drew attention to the rugged masculinity of his sharply angled jaw, square chin and his broad shoulders. Curls in the same dark shade dusted his powerfully built chest, and Juliana couldn't prevent her eyes from following the line of hair bisecting his well-defined abs to the button of his jeans.

"G'morning." His gravelly, sleep-roughened voice struck a match inside her, setting fire to her nerve endings as if they were fuses. She jerked her eyes upward and met his heavy-lidded gaze. He looked more like the big, bad wolf than ever and she wanted to be gobbled up by her reluctant rebel more with each passing day.

"Good morning."

She'd never spent an entire night in a man's bed—with or without him—and therefore, she'd never experienced a morning after. Was that why this felt so intimate and awkward? And yet she couldn't have left the room if she'd wanted to.

"Coffee?" He angled his head toward the pot on the counter.

"Please." Why couldn't she be one of those women who carried a makeup kit in her purse? She didn't even carry a comb or brush. She'd had to borrow his. Feeling unkempt and exposed, she dipped her head, swinging her hair over her cheek.

He filled a mug and passed it to her. "Milk? Sugar?"

She took it, being careful to avoid touching him. It was too early for that kind of shock to her system. "Just sugar."

He gestured toward the sugar bowl. "Help yourself."

"Thanks for um…washing my clothes." With the way her skin tingled, you'd think he'd handled her, not just her panties. The idea of becoming intimate with him was growing on her—almost enough to drown her remaining reservations about her crazy plan to break rules. Her hand shook as she sweetened the dark brew.

"You're welcome." He made no attempt to leave the kitchen. The room seemed to shrink and she had a hard time keeping her eyes off his body. If he'd lived a self-indulgent life before leaving Nashville as the tabloids claimed, then it didn't show. There wasn't an ounce of surplus flesh on his muscular torso.

She dragged her gaze from his pecs to his eyes. "Would you like for me to prepare breakfast?"

He scrubbed one hand across his nape. "I'm not sure what you'll find. I'm not a morning person. I usually don't eat until I go downstairs."

"May I search? The girls should eat before we head out. And honestly, there's not much food in my fridge either. I usually shop on Saturdays. Irma promised to bring lunch and snacks for the girls with her today."

"Go ahead." His assessing gaze slid over her, making her mouth dry and her palms dampen. She was out of her element and knew it. Not for the first time, she wished she had the sexual confidence of some of her coworkers, but the personal relationships in her past hadn't been the type to instill self-assurance. She opened the refrigerator and the cool air swept her hot cheeks.

She found eggs and butter in the fridge and then spotted bread on the counter. She located the pancake syrup in a cabinet. "French toast?"

"That'll work." His steady regard unnerved her. She tried to block him out as she mixed the batter, dunked the bread and laid it in the frying pan. What was he looking for?

He refilled his coffee cup. "You're not what I expected."

Ka-boom. Her heart pounded. She jerked up her chin. "Wh-why's that?"

"You dropped fifteen grand without batting an eyelash for lessons you could have bought for a fraction of that cost. I figured you had more money than sense."

Ouch. Talk about making a bad first impression.... "And now?"

"I was wrong."

The simple sentence filled her with an idiotic amount of pleasure. "Thank you."

"But that doesn't change the decision I made last night before Kelly showed up."

Uh-oh. She didn't like the sound of that. "Decision?"

"You need to take your lessons from someone else."

The bottom dropped out of her stomach. "Why?"

"Because I'm not looking for a short-term affair and you are."

Her lungs seized and mortification burned her face. "I *never* said that."

His mouth tilted in a skeptical slant. "Are you telling me you want to marry me?"

What! "No."

"But you're not averse to sleeping with me."

She gulped and focused intently on flipping the bread before meeting his gaze again. "What makes you think that?"

"Because you have a box of condoms in your purse."

Horrified, Juliana spun back to the stove. She prodded the French toast with the spatula even though it didn't need her immediate attention. "And how do you know that?"

"Because your purse was gaping open when I brought your clothes in this morning. The condoms were on top."

If she'd ever been more embarrassed, she couldn't recall the occasion, but she stood her ground. "You have quite an ego if you think they're for you."

Her snippy comment didn't faze him. Probably because it didn't come out in nearly as scathing a tone as she'd intended. How could it when he was right?

"That's what I thought, too, until I realized you're not the type of woman who picks up men."

"Don't be so sure," she blustered.

"You're an accountant."

"So?"

"So you like things neat, and you like to be prepared. The CDs in your car are arranged alphabetically. You memorize instruction manuals that most people don't even bother to read. You fasten your seat belt before putting the key in the ignition, and you check your mirrors three times before changing lanes. I'll bet you don't have a risk-taking bone in your body."

Boy did he have her pegged, and that annoyed her immensely. "I bought you, didn't I?"

"I'm guessing you researched my background before you did, because lady, you sure know a lot about me for someone who's not a country music fan."

Guilty as charged. If he'd noticed that her CDs were in alphabetical order then he'd probably also noticed she liked Broadway tunes. Little did he know she'd shoved his CDs under her seat before letting him into her car. "There's nothing wrong with being prepared."

"Never said there was. But the fact remains that what you want isn't available. I can't deny I need your help this week, but I'll arrange for you to take the rest of your lessons elsewhere."

She could concede to her embarrassment and his demands or she could stay the course she'd set. *Last chance. Last chance* echoed in her head. "Like you said, you owe me and I want my lessons from you. No substitutes."

Anger flared in his eyes and he opened his mouth—to argue probably—but snapped it shut again when the youngest of the girls toddled into the kitchen. She wordlessly held up her arms. Rex set down his coffee mug and scooped her up. "Hey, sweet pea."

The child popped a thumb in her mouth, laid her head on Rex's shoulder and then twirled a strand of his hair around the fingers of her opposite hand. The absolute trust in the gesture and the gentle kiss he planted on the child's crown brought a lump to Juliana's throat.

"Liza, this is Juliana. She's going to help me take care of you for a few days."

A pair of dark eyes briefly met Juliana's and then the child hid her face against Rex's neck. The tiny fingers tangled in Rex's hair wiggled in a wave and Juliana's heart melted. "Hi, Liza."

Juliana caught another peep from those shy eyes and smiled as she transferred the French toast onto plates. Kelly had told her Liza was three, Becky five and both girls adored their uncle. To hear Kelly talk last night, you'd think Rex was a big softie, but that wasn't the man Juliana had encountered.

"The girls must spend a lot of time with you."

He shrugged. "I try to help out when Mike's deployed."

An older girl bounced into the room and vaulted toward Rex. He caught her in his free arm so easily it was clear this was a common occurrence, and then he juggled a giggly girl on each hip. His smile nearly knocked Juliana's legs out from under her.

Seeing the obvious affection between Rex and his nieces turned her thoughts in a decidedly *un*temporary direction. She quickly squelched the unwelcome feelings. She'd never been one to listen for the ticking of her biological clock, and she didn't intend to start now. One month with the rebel was all she'd allow herself.

"This is Becky. Becky, Juliana is going to help out while Mom's away. You're going to spend the day at Juliana's house with her nanny."

"Hello, Becky."

The older girl studied Juliana suspiciously and then asked Rex, "Why? Why can't we stay here with you?"

"Because I have to work."

She might not have much experience with children, but Juliana could see the protests forming on that pouty lip and decided to head them off. "My town house has a pool and a playground, and Irma, the lady who took care of me when I was your age, is very excited about having young ladies to help her bake cookies."

Either the pool or the cookies did the trick. Both girls' eyes brightened. If only their uncle was as easy to bring around. Juliana stifled a sigh.

She had a plan and she would stick to it regardless of this slight detour. Despite Rex's avowed disinterest in a relationship, his kiss said otherwise, so her plan still had a chance. No one loved a tough case as much as she did, and she wasn't ready to throw in the towel yet.

She faced her reluctant seducer. "I need a key to your apartment."

And that, judging by Rex's balky expression, was the last thing he wanted to give her.

Five

Rex's life was spinning out of control—much like it had when he'd signed his first record deal, and others, his manager, his agent and the record company execs, had seized the wheel and started steering his life. He'd fought a long, hard battle to regain control, and he didn't like being knocked off track now.

Last night he'd been shanghaied by Kelly and Juliana. Today, Irma, as grandmotherly a woman as he'd ever met, had shooed him out of the way the moment he and the girls had arrived. She'd whisked Becky and Liza into the kitchen to help her unpack the groceries. Juliana had disappeared upstairs to dress for work, leaving him to prowl around her living room and wonder what in the hell he'd gotten into. Not that he'd had a choice. He wouldn't let Kelly down again.

Who was the real Juliana? The flirty siren who'd bought him at the auction, the innocent seductress who'd ridden his horse, the bold and sexy biker chick or the cautious woman who planned every detail and triple-checked everything? There were too many contradictions to count—contradictions that kept him off balance. He couldn't plan a defense if he didn't know his opponent.

Her living and dining rooms looked like something out of a magazine. Not fussy or cluttered, but decorated and comfortable. A soft toast-colored fabric covered the long sofa and matching chairs. The oversize furniture was the kind he could sink into and take a nap—which he sorely needed after tossing and turning on his shorter couch last night. A man could prop his boots on her wood-and-wrought-iron tables without worrying about scuffing the surface. The best part was that, other than a few colorful ceramic pieces on high shelves, Juliana didn't have valuable knickknacks all over the place that the girls could break.

A noise made him turn. He looked up and saw legs—amazing, long, sexy legs—coming down the stairs. And then the rest of Juliana came into view. In her gray body-skimming suit, twisted-up hair and low-heeled shoes, she bore little resemblance to any of the versions of Juliana he'd encountered thus far. This woman looked like a bank employee. Cool. Collected. In charge. The tap of her heels on the hardwood floor as she crossed to a cabinet drew his attention back to her killer legs.

Damned if he didn't find her sexy in a librarian kind of way. Not good. Not good at all.

She opened a drawer, withdrew something and then turned to face him. "Here's a key to my house."

Whoa. He backed up a step. Other than Kelly, he'd never given a woman keys to his place or even his truck. "Look, Juliana, I gave you my spare keys this morning because you and the girls need access to my apartment, but—"

"Yes, and it was clearly very painful for you," she said with a dose of sarcasm.

He shoved his hands in his pockets. "I don't need a key to your house."

"You will if you arrive before Irma in the mornings."

"I won't. I'll make sure of it. But if I do, you can let me in."

She shook her head and the tiny diamonds in her earlobes sparkled, drawing his attention to her delicate ears and the slender column of her neck above the collarless suit.

"That isn't practical. You live closer to the bank, so it makes more sense for me to go straight to work from Renegade. The earlier I can get to work, the sooner I can leave to be with the girls. Irma's thrilled to have them, but she's seventy, and she's worried that her stamina may not last a full day."

The skin between his shoulder blades prickled. No way out. Going into a woman's house without her... He suppressed a shudder. Swapping keys was *way* too intimate and smelled like a commitment. Commitments led to disappointments, and he'd already handed out more than his share of those. He wanted to unload Juliana and the unwelcome attraction for her, not add another loop to the rope temporarily binding them together.

Juliana reached out, grabbed his hand and pressed the key into his palm. She closed his fingers around the cool metal and squeezed. Her hands, wrapped securely around his, ignited desires he could not—would not—satisfy.

"Rex, it's a key ring not an engagement ring. There are no strings or expectations attached. Quit being such a *guy* and take it." She made being male sound like an insult. "I have to go. I'm running late."

But several seconds ticked past before her fingers loosened and her hands fell away. From the rapid flutter of her pulse at the base of her neck, he guessed he wasn't the only one feeling the heat generated by their exchange.

He cleared his throat. "I'll drop Becky and Liza off about 9:30 or 10:00 each morning."

She nodded. "I should be back by 6:00 at the latest. The girls and I will find you so you can tell them good night before I take them upstairs. You're welcome to stay here as long as you like. Irma makes great coffee."

This was so much like playing house, it gave him the willies. Knowing his past and his weakness, thinking about building a domestic relationship with someone was a luxury he couldn't afford. He backed up. "Right. See ya tonight."

And then he bolted for the kitchen like a damned coward. Running from what he couldn't have.

Wally Wilson was perfect for her on so many levels. So why couldn't Juliana be happy with him and forget this *last chance* nonsense?

She looked across the table at her companion. Handsome in an understated, preppy way, Wally was blond, blue-eyed and reasonably fit. He kept his skin evenly tanned with weekly visits to the tanning salon. Every hair stayed in place thanks to his skilled barber, and wrinkles didn't dare crease his suit.

No, women wouldn't get whiplash or have hormone surges when he walked through a room, but he was stable, responsible and unfailingly polite. He liked order and so did she. In fact, they had so much in common. Background, business, ambition…

As detail-oriented as Wally appeared to be about everything else in his life, he would probably be a conscientious lover. According to her friends, Juliana owed it to herself to find out before marrying him, but the idea didn't fill her with anticipation. Then again, she hated emotional displays. Life with Wally would be smooth sailing. No highs. No lows.

No fun?

She ignored that pesky inner voice and smiled at Wally. "Thank you for agreeing to switch our date from dinner to lunch on such short notice, Wally."

"I'm always happy to accommodate your schedule, Juliana. What did you say came up?"

She hadn't said and she didn't understand her hesitation in revealing the situation now, but if she was seriously considering marrying him, then they shouldn't have secrets between them. "I'm babysitting this evening."

His brows lifted. "Babysitting? Have you ever babysat before?"

"Um…no. But the girls are three and five. I'm sure they can tell me if I do something wrong."

"I thought it might have something to do with your bachelor."

Her chicken salad lodged halfway down her esophagus. She sipped her water. "It does indirectly. Rex—my bachelor—Rex's sister had to fly out of the country unexpectedly. Her husband's in the military, and he's been critically injured. She needed to be with him. Rex and I are watching their children."

"Couldn't she hire someone to do that?"

"Irma's helping."

"Ah, yes. Irma. I'd forgotten you still keep in touch with your nanny." He flashed a tolerant smile, displaying perfectly aligned teeth. Why did she get the impression he didn't really approve of her continued friendship with the woman who'd raised her while Margaret Alden had fought her way up the career ladder?

"Irma and I have lunch together at least once a month. I've been increasingly concerned about her lately. Retirement isn't working out." He nodded, but she had the impression he really didn't care about Irma. Juliana pleated her napkin in her lap. "Wally, my mother seems to think you expected me to buy you at the auction."

"Given the understanding between our families, I thought you might," he said in an expressionless tone. Come to think of it, Wally usually spoke without much inflection. His soothing voice would be an asset in dealing with upset customers.

"The understanding was that we'd date to see if we suited."

"Don't we?"

She concealed a wince. "I don't know yet, Wally, but please tell Donna I appreciate her stepping in. Although I confess I was a little surprised to see her at the club."

"Yes. There are those who can't forget Donna's humble beginnings."

Like his parents, Juliana suspected. Mrs. Wilson referred to Wally's administrative assistant as "trailer trash." His father called Donna worse. The Wilsons saw a gold digger out to sink her claws into the family fortune. Never mind that Donna had worked hard to get her GED and then had attended community college while raising a houseful of children single-handedly. Wally's mother couldn't see Donna's ambition or intelligence. Juliana, on the other hand, often teased Wally that she wanted to steal his assistant.

"Well, I apologize if I've made things difficult for you."

"No apologies are necessary, Juliana. In fact, this could work to our advantage."

"How so?"

"Because we're each being allowed to date outside our closed social circle without fear of repercussion."

That had to be the oddest comment she'd ever heard Wally make. Even stranger was the inkling that Wally—safe, sensible Wally—might have secrets.

Rex let himself into his apartment and stopped in his tracks when he spotted Juliana slumped in one corner of the sofa with her knees bent and her feet tucked beside her.

His heart thumped like a bass drum as he drew nearer. The lamp cast a soft glow over her sleep-flushed face. Dark lashes fanned her cheeks and her lips parted on a sigh of breath. She'd exchanged her suit for a pair of sleeveless pajamas. The black fabric reminded him of the satin sheets he'd had on his tour bus. Soft. Slippery. *Sexy.*

Shaking off the forbidden thought, he glanced down the hall. Through the open door, the soft glow of a night-light revealed the sleeping girls. Had they given Juliana a hard time? Was that why she'd planted herself out here like a sentry? Or had she fallen asleep waiting for him? The thought sent a streak of lightning sizzling through him. She'd made it clear that she wanted him with her insistence on the lessons and with that damned box of condoms. He'd thought of little else all day.

It would be so easy to take what she offered, to lead her to bed and lose himself in the spicy floral scent of her skin and the slick warmth of her body. For an hour or two she could make him feel like something more than a washed-up country singer who'd let his family down in all the ways that counted. Sure, he'd started sending money home as soon as he'd signed his first contract, but he'd never sent more than cold cash, and he'd never apologized for hurting the two people who'd loved him the most. Mindless sex could cure a lot of things—including guilt—for a while. He ought to know.

He fisted his hands against the urge to stroke Juliana into wakefulness. Oh yeah. It would be so easy to be that selfish SOB with her. And that was exactly why he had to keep his distance. He couldn't go back, couldn't risk letting Kelly and the girls down the way he'd let his folks down.

But Juliana being out here instead of in his bed could work to his advantage. He'd take a shower and wash away the temptation along with the food and bar smells, and then he'd wake Juliana and send her to his bed. Alone.

As quietly as possible, Rex entered his room to collect

fresh clothing. The sight of her suits lined up beside his jeans in the closet rattled him. He extracted what he needed and headed for the bathroom, only to receive another shock. Her toiletries neatly lined the counter and her shampoo stood next to his in the shower stall.

Yesterday, he'd wanted to get away from her. *Today, she'd moved in.* Oh yeah, his life was definitely veering out of control, but he'd learned the hard way how destructive that could be. It wasn't a mistake he'd repeat.

He stripped off his clothing, stepped into the shower and lathered briskly, valiantly fighting traitorous thoughts of Juliana's soap-slickened hands gliding over his skin, but he was too tired to maintain his mental barricades. In seconds, he had a painful hard-on begging for attention. He twisted the faucet to cold and shivered in the bone-jarring, frigid water while he rinsed off the soap and shampoo. After toweling off and pulling on clean jeans and a T-shirt, he set his shoulders. Time to put temptation to bed and try to catch some shut-eye before this merry-go-round started again tomorrow. Saturday. Juliana's day off. How would he concentrate on work knowing she was in his apartment all day?

He stopped beside the sofa and struggled with the bite of awareness. He couldn't forget the softness of her skin or the taste of her mouth. Dammit. He couldn't remember ever getting turned on so fast or having a woman haunt his thoughts day and night. Had to be the celibacy screwing with his head.

One week. He could hold out until Kelly returned home and then, debt or no debt, he'd dump Juliana.

"Juliana," he whispered. She didn't stir. He didn't want to raise his voice and risk waking the girls. "Juliana, wake up."

Nothing. Damn. He'd have to touch her. But where? The bare skin of her shoulder was too close to the shadowy area between her breasts. Too risky. He patted her kneecap. "Juliana."

She startled, inhaled a quick breath and jerked upright. "What? Oh, hello."

"Go to bed."

She blinked owlishly and scanned the room as if she couldn't remember where she was or how she'd gotten there. She looked flustered and adorable and kissable. Damn.

She shoved her hair out of her face. "The girls?"

"Asleep."

She yawned and her breasts lifted beneath her satiny shirt. "Becky had a nightmare. I guess I dozed off."

The quiet statement struck with the sudden impact of a rock hitting his truck's windshield. A crack slowly snaked through the resistance he fought so hard to maintain. "Nice of you to listen out for her."

What was it about her that fueled his engine like nobody else had? He'd met prettier women, women with bigger boobs and longer legs. But he couldn't remember one from his past who got to him this way, let alone one who'd have volunteered for the non-glamorous, tough job of babysitting somebody else's kids. Not that he'd ever known any of his past lovers that well.

Slowly, she unfolded and stood, and then she stumbled and fell against his chest. He caught her upper arms. Her fingers splayed over his heart. She couldn't miss the rapid-fire beat.

Her slumberous gaze lifted to his. "Sorry. My foot's asleep."

And not one single, sorry cell in his body was. His hands tightened. He wanted her so bad, he ached with it. Wanted to taste her damp lips. Wanted to caress her flushed skin. Wanted to bury his face in the valley between her breasts and make her as hungry for him as he was for her. Wanted to push her back on the sofa and bury himself between her long legs.

What would it hurt? It's what she wants prompted the selfish bastard lurking inside him.

Rex's jaw muscles protested his tooth-gritting abuse, and

he battled with the throbbing need he should have satisfied in the shower. No, it wouldn't have been as good as the real thing, but he could have taken the edge off his craving.

User. An icy drop of water from his wet hair snaked down his spine, shocking him into clearheadedness. He set her away, holding on only until he was sure she had her footing.

"Go to bed, Juliana."

All dressed up and no place to go.

Juliana paced Rex's bedroom. An early riser by habit, she'd awoken without an alarm. She needed coffee immediately and a newspaper soon. Today's edition should contain Octavia Jenkins's first installment about the auction. Juliana didn't want to wake Rex or the girls by running the sputtering coffee machine, and she didn't know if he subscribed to the local paper.

Clutching her key to the apartment and her wallet, she eased open the bedroom door. As silently as possible, she tiptoed into the den. Her heart stalled when she spotted Rex sprawled on the sofa and then raced as her gaze drank him in. His shiny hair spilled over the cappuccino-colored leather like bittersweet chocolate drizzled over milk chocolate. His bare feet hung over the opposite end. He'd shed his shirt and unbuttoned the top button on his jeans. The sheet he'd used lay puddled on the floor beside him. Her gaze returned to that unfastened brass button and the shadow of his navel behind it, and then raked over his bare chest to his bristly chin and parted lips.

Her mouth dried. He definitely knew how to use those lips. The question was how did she get him to use them again. On her. With each encounter, her desire to be held against that broad hair-spattered chest grew and her ambivalence over this crazy scheme faded, but she didn't appear to be getting any closer to her goal, so her uncertainty was a moot point.

What was she going to do to tempt him next, and how far could she go with the girls in the house?

She tiptoed to the girls' door and found them sleeping peacefully. Her heart twinged a little. She'd never expected to enjoy caring for them so much. They were sweet and funny and obviously adored their uncle. Unfortunately, Juliana was getting a bit too fond of their uncle as well. The idea of one month of naughty thrills and then a quick goodbye didn't sound nearly as attractive as it once had. In fact, she wondered if one month would be enough.

She wanted to know more about Rex Tanner than her online searches had revealed. Like what put those shadows in his dark eyes? And what had driven a man at the top of his career to self-destruct? Unfortunately, the girls couldn't tell her and Rex wouldn't.

Rex slept through her examination, but that was understandable since he'd only come upstairs four hours ago. Juliana eased through his apartment door—the one leading to the exterior stairs instead of through Renegade—aiming for the coffee shop she'd spotted down the street yesterday. The early morning humidity clung to her skin on the short walk. She purchased her caffeine fix and a newspaper and headed back to Rex's, where she settled at the picnic table on his upstairs deck overlooking the Cape Fear River.

The sun had risen high enough at 6:30 for her to read the newsprint, but not high enough to bake her skin. She wasn't one of those women who tanned well. She turned an unbecoming shade of boiled-shrimp pink, but she'd forgotten to pack her sunscreen. She'd have to retreat inside in a few minutes—back to the space dominated by Rex. And she didn't think she could handle him without a full load of caffeine in her system.

With her back to the house, she flipped straight to the Lifestyles section, found Octavia's byline and winced at the title of the article: Love at Any Price? She quickly scanned over the introductory info. Her eyes skidded to a halt when she found her name, and then she backtracked and began the paragraph again.

Bachelor nine. Rex Tanner and Juliana Alden each claim to have pure motives for participating in the auction. The former Nashville headliner says all he wants is publicity for Renegade, his new waterfront bar and grill. Ms. Alden declares her interests lie in the motorcycle lessons. But this reporter believes the relationship will yield more than improved revenues and riding skills. The sparks between the dashing biker and the proper banker nearly set the room ablaze.

Appalled, Juliana dropped the paper on the table and pressed cold hands to her hot cheeks. Was she so obvious? Everyone in Wilmington would know she was pursuing Rex. Everyone including her mother and Wally. The fallout from that would not be pleasant. Her mouth dried and panic made her heart palpitate erratically. She'd wanted a month of breaking rules, not a month of public embarrassment.

She dug her cell phone out of her pocket and hit speed dial. "H'lo," Andrea answered in a groggy voice.

"Andrea, I'm sorry if I woke you, but I've just read Octavia Jenkins's article. It's awful."

A groan carried over the phone line. "You didn't wake me. I've seen it. Oh my God. 'This romance is ready to be rekindled. Is Ms. Montgomery carrying the matches?' I am so *not* trying to win Clay back. I'm going to ask Octavia to print a retraction."

Juliana grimaced. She'd been so concerned with her own predicament she hadn't even read about Andrea or Holly. She scanned down the page and read the section Andrea had quoted. "I don't think you'll get a retraction. She hasn't really crossed the line."

"Says you."

"Did you see what she wrote about Rex and me? Now everyone knows what I'm doing. And if that's not humiliating enough, guess what? It's not working. You said he was such a womanizer that all I'd have to do was show up and keep breathing and he'd do the rest. Well, he's not doing it."

"What are you talking about?"

Juliana shot a quick, cautious glance over her shoulder and then whispered, "Getting Rex to seduce me."

"He's not interested?"

"He's interested...at least I think he is, but I... I wanted someone who would sweep me off my feet and overcome my doubts about this whole crazy scheme. He's not sweeping."

"Men are so obtuse. You're going to have to nudge him in the right direction. Let's meet for breakfast and plot our way out of this mess. I'll call Holly and tell her to meet us at Magnolia's Diner."

"I can't."

"Why?"

"Because I'm babysitting Rex's nieces today."

"Babysitting? No, no, no. Juliana, kids and sex don't mix. I'm coming over. We need to talk."

She took a fortifying gulp of coffee. "You can't come over because I'm not at home."

"Where are you?"

She hesitated and then confessed. "Staying at Rex's apartment above Renegade."

Silent seconds ticked past. "I'm sure there's a good explanation why you're living with him and not getting any? Besides the children, I mean."

Tapping drew Juliana's gaze to the girls' bedroom window. Two angelic faces grinned out at her. She smiled back and waved, and then pressed her finger to her lips in the universal Be quiet sign. "It's complicated, but I can't explain now. I have to go."

"You can't leave me hanging like that," Andrea squawked.

"Sorry. Have to. Bye." She disconnected over Andrea's protests, gathered her paper, coffee and keys and let herself inside.

"Man, you're driving me crazy, and your prowling is scaring off customers. Go away."

Rex frowned at Danny. "I thought I was the boss."

"Rex, I can handle this crowd. Go check on the girls or the chick or whoever's got your nuts in a knot."

Rex had never been more conscious of the empty apartment over his head. Dammit, it was supposed to be empty. He liked living alone. But he'd been out of sorts since yesterday morning when he'd awoken to silence. How had Juliana sneaked the girls out without waking him? Probably because sleep was next to impossible knowing he had a sexy *and willing* banker in his bed, and when he'd finally drifted off he'd dreamed of the bedroom door opening and Juliana beckoning him to join her. In his dreams, he hadn't refused her invitation. Heat pulsed through him.

He'd found a note from Juliana in the kitchen saying she'd taken the girls to her place, and that she'd like for them to spend Saturday night with her so they wouldn't disturb him. He was supposed to call her cell phone if he didn't like the idea. He hadn't liked the idea, but he couldn't explain why, so he hadn't called. One day less exposure to Juliana was one day he didn't have to fight the pull between them. No doubt the girls would love a sleepover. He should be grateful. But he wasn't.

The newspaper Juliana had left on his kitchen table hadn't improved his mood. Sure, the auction article had generated additional business as he'd hoped. They'd had the best weekend crowd yet, but too many customers had asked him about his romance with Juliana. They wanted a freaking fairy-tale ending and that wasn't going to happen. She might be a banking princess, but he'd proven he wasn't prince material.

He finished wiping down the bar and pitched his rag into the bucket of cleaning solution. "I didn't expect her to keep Becky and Liza at her place all weekend."

"What are you complaining about? You got your bed back, and she and the squirts aren't underfoot." Danny didn't have kids of his own, but he still lived at home and he had a gaggle of younger siblings whom he claimed were always in the way. "Go."

Rex glanced at his watch. Five o'clock. If he left now, he'd have time to take a quick shower and then play with the girls before dinner. "All right. I'm going. Call Juliana's if you need me. Number's by the phone."

Forty minutes later, he parked his truck in the driveway beside Juliana's sedan, climbed the stairs and rang her doorbell. No one responded to the bell or his knock, but using his key was too damned domesticated for him. He walked around to the back of the end-unit town house, but the girls weren't on the patio, and he couldn't see them through the French doors. Damn. He dug his key out of his pocket and let himself in. Using the key did *not* mean he and Juliana had a relationship beyond the girls and the lessons.

"Juliana? Becky? Liza?" Silence echoed back.

Bottles of nail polish stood like a line of candy-colored fence posts on the kitchen table, corralling a neat pile of hair ribbons and an assortment of other girlie stuff. Juliana's purse leaned against a stack of child-care and babysitting books on the hall table. That she cared enough to try to learn more about his nieces shouldn't get to him, but it did.

How could he have been so wrong in his initial assessment that she had more money than brains? He shrugged off his growing admiration. The last thing he needed was to soften up around her. Liking her and appreciating her generosity didn't change the fact that he was in debt up to his neck to her family, or that she was looking for a walk on the wild side and he wasn't. She wanted excitement and he wanted...

What did he want? Roots? Maybe. He scrubbed a hand over the back of his neck. One of these days, when the bar was on a firmer footing, he wouldn't mind having someone to come home to, but he'd made more than his share of mistakes and let a lot of people down. He shook his head. Even if he did decide to take a chance—one he was sure he'd blow—on something long-term, a banking heiress wouldn't be interested in anything permanent from a long-haired biker with a highway education and a wardrobe consisting of jeans and T-shirts with the Renegade logo on the back. She'd end up with a college-educated *GQ* guy in a suit. A man like the other bachelors at the charity auction.

Juliana and the girls couldn't be far if her purse and car were here. He locked up and headed for the playground. Excited, happy squeals made him detour toward the nearby pool. A couple of dozen folks populated the fenced area. Becky's rebel yell drew his gaze to the shallow end. She launched herself from the side of the pool and hit the water with a decent splash, but bobbed back to the surface thanks to a new hot-pink life jacket. Next, he spotted Liza, also sporting a new life jacket in smiley-face yellow, her favorite color. She dog-paddled toward a slender, dark-haired woman whose mostly bare back faced him.

Juliana. He didn't need to see her face to recognize her.

Every male hormone in his body pointed her out like a hunting dog signaled quail. The line of her naked spine and the curve of her waist in the hip-deep water brought a flood of moisture to his mouth and kicked his heart into a staccato beat. Her two-piece swimsuit wasn't skimpy by today's standards, but knowing only a few scraps of fabric separated him from her bare skin hit him with the blast of a spotlight. Sweat oozed from his pores. His black shirt and jeans magnified his reaction by absorbing every hot ray of the evening sunshine. Her low and husky laugh at Becky's antics only increased his discomfort.

Juliana ducked under the water, and Liza squealed and squirmed with joy and then cackled when Juliana shot out of the water, slicked back her hair and gently splashed Becky. Apparently, the banker had a playful side and the urge to play with her was getting damned hard for Rex to ignore. He gripped the white picket fence and struggled to corral his stampeding hormones.

"Uncle Rex!" Becky yelled.

Cover blown. He gritted a smile, ordered his body to behave and shoved open the gate. Juliana jerked around to face him and he nearly tripped over a seam in the sidewalk. Her breasts were round, pale, perfect and far too exposed in a blue top the exact shade of her eyes for his peace of mind.

"Wook, Unca Wex." Liza's voice drew his attention away from forbidden territory. "I swimmen."

"And doing a great job of it, sweet pea. Hey, Beck, killer cannonball." Becky responded by hauling herself out of the pool and launching another one, this one soaking him. He welcomed the cool water on his overheated skin.

"We've had a busy day." Juliana's quiet words forced him to look at her again—something he'd rather not do until she covered up from ears to ankles. "They should sleep well tonight."

At the sight of all that creamy, curvaceous flesh on display, words failed him. He grunted an affirmative.

"Is something wrong? You're supposed to be working." She folded her arms across her middle, which should have helped his concentration since it covered a lot of skin, but the move pushed her breasts farther out of her suit, resulting in a negative effect on his brain function. It took him a few seconds to weed her question out of his testosterone-induced fog.

"Danny's closing. I thought I'd take the girls out to dinner and then head back to my place. Tomorrow's my day off, so I'll keep 'em tonight and you can sleep in your own bed." He glanced at Becky and Liza in time to see their faces fall.

Juliana waded toward the pool steps. "We'd planned to grill kebabs tonight, and we've made homemade ice cream. Why don't you join us for dinner?"

Bad idea. How could he get out of it? "Kebabs?"

"We stuck 'em," Liza said in as bloodthirsty a tone as he'd ever heard from a three-year-old. He grabbed her upraised hands, lifted her from the pool and set her on the concrete.

Juliana bit her lip, but she couldn't hide the smile twitching on her mouth. The mischievous sparkle in her eyes slammed the breath right out of him. "The girls helped me assemble the kebabs. We bought the ice-cream freezer when we bought the life jackets. Cooking together seemed like a good activity."

"Right. Dinner sounds good." *Liar, liar, pants on fire.*

Becky vaulted out and gave him a soggy hug. He ruffled her wet hair with a surprisingly unsteady hand.

Juliana rose from the pool like a nymph in a wet dream. Rivulets of water cascaded over the peaks and valleys of a truly lust-worthy body. His throat closed and his skin ignited. The little flirty skirt of her bathing suit bottom stopped an inch below her navel, and the wet fabric clung to her hips like a second skin.

He exhaled slowly and turned his back on what he couldn't have to help the girls dry off. The week ahead yawned like an eternity.

"Wook." Liza lifted her hands. He blinked away the sensual haze clouding his vision, knelt beside Liza and focused on her tiny, pale pink-tipped nails. "Oo-liana painted dem."

"Pretty."

Juliana stopped beside them. Her toenails bore the same shade of polish. Rex fought the urge to trace the long, lean line of her legs with his gaze and lost. From his kneeling position on the concrete, the sight of those perfect breasts at eye level wreaked no end of havoc below his belt. Frustration and futility rose inside him.

Surrender man and be done with it.

No way. Too much to lose.

He stood and met the gaze of the woman determined to bring him to his knees. Damned if she didn't have him like a fish on the hook, and fighting the line wasn't getting him anywhere but reeled in and too tired to care. Unless he wanted to be left on the dock gasping for air, then he had to do something fast.

But he had a feeling it was too late.

Six

Rex prowled around Juliana's den like a caged animal. Examining an item here, looking out a window there, but never remaining still for more than a few seconds.

With her senses hyperaware of each shift of his muscular frame, Juliana sipped her favorite locally produced peach wine and tugged at the hem of the sundress she'd changed into after returning from the pool.

The fuchsia dress had hung in her closet unworn for years because the bodice dipped lower than she liked, and the hem was inches higher than comfortable. She'd bought it and the ridiculously high-heeled matching sandals for a cruise she, Andrea and Holly had scheduled to celebrate their twenty-seventh birthdays but had never taken due to Juliana's emergency appendectomy.

"I'll repay you for everything you've spent on Irma, the life jackets, the doll clothes, whatever. How much do I owe ya?" Rex's gaze raked her exposed skin for the third time. He glanced away and looked again, convincing Juliana that her sexy dress was worth every penny she'd paid for it even if she never wore it again.

She crossed her legs and then smoothed her hem. Rex's eyes tracked each movement. Hmm. Interesting. Leaning forward, she deposited her wineglass on the coffee table and hooked a finger beneath the thin gold chain at her neck. Rex's dark eyes fastened on the stroke of her fingers inside the V-neck of her bodice. His Adam's apple bobbed.

A sense of feminine power swelled inside her. He *was* attracted to her. What would it take to break through his restraint? *C'mon, bad boy, corrupt me.*

What had he said again? Oh, yes. "Your sister is covering Irma's salary. The rest…" She shrugged and gestured to where Becky and Liza played dress-up with their dolls in the corner. "It's my pleasure. The girls and I are having fun."

"I insist."

"Your sister said you would. The answer's still no, Rex." She kicked her ankle just a little, dangling the sandal from her toes just to see if he'd watch. He did. She bit the inside of her lip to stop a pleased smile.

His fists clenched and unclenched. "Kelly called this morning. Mike made it through surgery and he's stable. Now it's a wait-and-see game, but the doctors are optimistic."

She uncrossed her legs and shifted on the sofa. The move inched her hem higher—a bonus she hadn't anticipated. "For Kelly and the girls' sake I hope he pulls through."

"Yeah." The word was little more than a grunt. His gaze never left her legs.

"Are you sure you don't want some wine? I'm sorry I don't have beer." She leaned forward to retrieve her glass and savored the shift of his eyes to her cleavage. Her nipples tightened.

A femme fatale is born. The incongruity of the statement nearly made her laugh out loud. She loved the way Rex's hot glances made her feel all restless and warm. Parts of her body tingled that had never tingled before.

"No thanks."

Sometimes an account investigation led her in a surprising direction. She'd learned to trust her instincts and go with it. "Then could you stop pacing and sit down?" She patted the cushion beside her. "You're making the girls nervous."

A lie. The girls had quit watching him circle the room ten minutes ago, but each pass of those lean hips through her line of vision pushed her closer to sensory overload. My gosh, she was ogling him and his um…parts, and she really wanted to know if he lived up to the promise in those jeans. Her bold thoughts made her cheeks burn.

He lowered himself into a chair on the opposite side of the coffee table, rested his elbows on his knees and then propped his head in his hands. Juliana studied his thick hair, the tense line of his shoulders and tightened her fingers around the stem of her wineglass instead of reaching across the distance to touch him the way she wanted. She'd never considered herself a sensual or tactile person, but the better she got to know Rex, the harder it was to resist the urge to touch him. His sleek hair. His rough jaw. His hard muscles.

She didn't lack initiative in her professional life, but in her personal life she'd definitely be classified as a slow-starter. In light of Rex's reaction tonight, she almost looked forward to making a move. Almost.

He lifted his head suddenly and his coffee-colored eyes pinned her in place. "Why me? The truth this time."

The wine in her glass sloshed over her fingers. Stalling, she dabbed at the liquid with a tissue. He wouldn't accept an evasive answer this time, she'd bet, and she wasn't a gambling person. Her gaze flicked to the girls in the corner. How much did she dare explain? "Because I have a nice life."

"What?" He sounded as if he thought she'd lost her mind.

"I'm thirty years old. I have a nice car, a nice home and a nice job. *Nice* is bland and boring. Like me. I hoped your auction package might jar me out of my 'nice' rut. There has to be more to life than *nice,* and if there is I don't want to miss out."

Wary understanding softened his eyes and then he leaned back in the chair and clasped his hands over his flat belly—a relaxed pose, but the intense look in his eyes was anything but relaxed. "I used to want more, too. And then I realized that *more* wasn't as great as it sounded."

She savored the tiny insight into his thoughts. "Your music career?"

Seconds ticked past as he studied his knotted fingers. "Yeah. I couldn't wait to get off that ranch and be somebody besides Reed Tanner's boy. Then I was. And everybody wanted me to be somebody else."

"I don't understand."

"The record execs, my manager and my publicist signed me because I was different. And then they tried to turn me into a carbon copy of every other guy on the charts."

"But you made it to the top without sounding like everyone else." She wasn't a country music fan, so her comparison wasn't firsthand, but she'd read the online articles touting Rex's unique sound and fresh way with words, and she enjoyed his music.

"I made it because I fought 'em every step of the way. The point is, you don't have to try to be somebody you're not."

But who was she exactly? Until the pressure to marry Wally had come about, Juliana had been certain she knew. For as far back as she could remember, she'd been groomed to take her place in the Alden Bank executive offices. That goal had always taken precedence over anything and anyone else. And she'd been happy with that decision. A life without emotional ups and downs suited her. She'd had a ringside seat when Andrea had fallen head-over-heels in love and when her friend had crash-landed with a broken heart. Afterward, Juliana had considered guarding her heart and avoiding the same kind of pain a good idea.

But now she had her doubts. Look at Irma. Her former nanny had dedicated herself to a career of caring for other women's children. Now that age had forced Irma to retire from the job that had defined her, what did she have left? Nothing. No family. No hobbies. Juliana didn't want to be left with nothing, but she wasn't sure meekly falling in with her mother's plans was the answer.

The foundation she'd built her life on was shaking and she didn't know if it would settle or crumble beneath her.

She lifted her gaze to the man in front of her. "Was fighting for what you wanted worth it?"

If it had been, then why had he left his dreams behind?

He shot to his feet. "Becoming my own man was a journey I had to take, but I was selfish. I hurt people along the way. And I let 'em down. I shouldn't have."

Who had he let down? And how?

Before she could ask, he turned to Becky and Liza. "Girls, we gotta go. Get your stuff and say good night."

Juliana wanted to dig deeper, but in the hustle to gather the girls' belongings there wasn't time or opportunity for questions. She walked the trio to Rex's truck and helped buckle the girls into their car seats. First Liza and then Becky insisted on giving her a hug and kiss good-night, and the gestures tugged at Juliana's heart.

"Thanks for dinner," he said as he started the truck.

Juliana stepped back, folded her arms and watched them

drive out of sight. Would she ever have children? The odds didn't favor her chances. At thirty years old, she'd never come close to finding a man with whom she wanted to spend the rest of her life. Sure, she'd had relationships, but her dedication to her job had always outweighed her commitment to the man in question, and none of her dates had ever interested her enough to make her want to leave work early or take a day off. If not for Andrea and Holly, she'd probably never take a vacation.

If you marry Wally, you could have children. Yet another plus in the Wally column. So why couldn't she just agree to the engagement and be done with it? Why vacillate? Was she being unrealistic to want more than a good rapport with her spouse? Was true intimacy a fallacy perpetuated by romantic books and movies? And was she even capable of letting someone get that close?

Juliana's office door burst open Monday just before lunch. She marked her place on the ledger with a finger and glanced up. Her mother's scowl turned Juliana's stomach into a hornet's nest. Clearly, the avoidance punishment had ended. "Hello, Mother."

Margaret Alden slapped a newspaper onto Juliana's desk. "This is outrageous."

The Saturday edition lay open to Octavia Jenkins's column, "Love at Any Price?" Juliana masked a wince. So much for hoping her mother would miss the article. "Octavia is trying to sell papers, and she's supporting your pet charity. Did you notice she gave the address to which donations can be mailed?"

"Have you read this? Do you realize the damage she's done to your engagement?"

Juliana should have known her mother wouldn't ask her if she had feelings for Rex or if the column was off base. They'd never had that kind of relationship. No, Juliana had shared her confidences with Irma, Andrea and Holly.

"I'm not engaged yet, and if you read the entire article, then you'll see that Octavia has also implied a romantic entanglement between Wally and Donna and Eric and Holly."

Juliana had hated reading about her brother and her best friend, and she hoped Octavia had her facts wrong, and yet Juliana was afraid to call Holly and find out. "You know those aren't true."

"I certainly hope Eric isn't involved with Holly. She has disappointed her parents terribly by living out in that shack like a bohemian."

"It's not a shack. It's a restored farmhouse and her studio." She'd said the words so many times before they came out in a singsong chorus.

"And Wallace knows better. That woman is not one of us."

The snobbery offended Juliana. She should have been used to it by now since she'd heard it her entire life. "You mean she wasn't born wealthy and didn't have everything handed to her on a silver platter?"

Her mother's nose lifted. "You and Eric didn't have everything handed to you."

"Yes, we did, Mother. Everything except respect, which we've had to fight an uphill battle to earn." *And our parents' attention, which seemed connected to perfect behavior,* Juliana added silently. The friends she'd had in school who'd dared to disobey had been shipped off to boarding school. Juliana had always followed the rules for fear of being sent away from Irma, Andrea, Holly and home.

"I'm calling the newspaper to have Ms. Jenkins removed from this series."

Juliana sighed and pushed back an errant strand of hair. "Sex sells, Mother. Octavia is doing her job."

"Are you saying you're having sex with that…that man?"

A rush of heat swept Juliana's face. "No, but even if I were sleeping with Rex, it wouldn't be any of your business."

"Don't make it my business by ruining this merger. By this time next year, Alden-Wilson will be the largest privately held bank in the southeast, and I will be the CEO."

"Only if Mr. Wilson is willing to step aside, and from what Wally has said, his father's not all that interested in being second in command. Mother, you may not win this one." Juliana admired her mother's ambition. All her life, she'd heard tales of how Margaret Alden had had it all—husband, family and career. Juliana wanted it all, too.

A smug smile curved her mother's lips. "Let me worry about that. You worry about making amends with Wallace. And make sure this little hussy isn't encroaching on your territory. Don't let me down, Juliana. This merger is far too important for you to jeopardize it with an unsuitable fling. Are we clear?"

She stalked out of Juliana's office as abruptly as she'd entered it.

Juliana sat back in her chair. *Don't let me down.* The battle cry of her life. But this time the feeling that the merger might be more important to her mother than Juliana's life and happiness unsettled her.

The suffocating straitjacket feeling that had driven her to buying the baddest bachelor on the block closed in on her, squeezing her ribs and compressing her lungs.

Last chance. Last chance.

She had to get out of here. She closed the ledger, withdrew her purse from her desk drawer and locked up. On the way out, she paused by her administrative assistant's desk. "I'm leaving for the day."

And then she turned her back on the woman's gaping mouth, walked out into the afternoon sunshine, took a deep breath of the hot, humid air and tasted freedom.

Trapped in his own damned apartment.

Rex knew he could lie, claim he had business downstairs and escape, leaving Juliana to listen for the girls. But he wasn't a coward. In the past, his failure to face his mistakes had cost him. He wouldn't run again. He'd agreed to the auction, agreed to keep the girls. That meant any fallout from those choices was his and his alone.

But damn. A man could only take so much, and his resistance had been slipping since Juliana had surprised him and the girls at the barn this afternoon with a picnic lunch. She'd spent the next four hours laughing, teasing and playing with Liza and Becky, and he'd discovered yet another facet to the formerly uptight auditor. A side he liked too much.

Restless, edgy and as horny as hell, he paced his den. A beautiful woman wanted him. The feeling was mutual. Why did he keep fighting the hunger that chewed him from the inside out? Because sleeping with Juliana would be mixing business with pleasure. Always a bad idea. But more important was that giving in to the craving inside him would open the door to his biggest weakness.

But he ached for her. The smell of her. The taste of her. The feel of her. Wrapped around him. Just once.

Fool. Having a little sex with Juliana is about as safe as a recovering alcoholic taking just one drink. You'll be sucked back into the world that almost destroyed you so fast you'll never recover.

Juliana stepped out of the girls' bedroom and closed the door. Rex's stomach hit the soles of his boots.

She looked like a combination of angel and siren with her

sable hair hanging loose. The strands teased her bare shoulders and the cleavage revealed by a fragile, fluttery pale blue top that ended a couple of inches above low-rider jeans. A wide woven belt circled her hips with its tasseled ties swaying over no-man's-land with every hypnotizing stride she took toward him. Those tassels affected his libido like a flashing neon Come and Get It sign.

He dragged his gaze up to the half smile on her face. Trouble. Pure trouble. Sweat oozed from his pores, dampening his upper lip, chest and back. His heart drummed harder, faster. His breathing turned shallow.

"The girls are out for the night."

Her whisper sent a bead of sweat snaking down his spine. He suppressed a shiver. "You should turn in. Early start tomorrow."

"It's only nine. Why don't you put on some music?" She sank onto the sofa and crossed her legs. She'd removed her shoes at some point. Her pink-tipped toes wiggled, and the lamp reflected off a gold toe ring on her right second toe and glittered on an ankle bracelet.

Oh, man. He swallowed, but his mouth remained as dry as a dust bowl. "No stereo."

She blinked. "You don't own a stereo? Isn't that a little unusual given your previous occupation?"

"Music's no longer a part of my life."

"Why?"

For a lot of reasons, none of which he'd share. "No time."

"Was it hard to walk away from something you loved?"

Dammit. Why did she insist on getting inside his head? Every time they met, she peppered him with questions. "No."

Liar. There were times—like today, *like now*—when feelings bottled up inside him and his fingers twitched for his guitar so he could pour out those emotions. As a teen and later as an adult, he'd worked through his tangled thoughts with music, singing, writing lyrics or just playing melodies long into the night. Sometimes he'd thought music was the only thing that kept him sane.

The more time he spent with Juliana, the more his thoughts strayed to the old Fender in the back of his closet. But he wouldn't pull out the instrument, wouldn't let her force him back into that world. A world that had cost him his family, his home, his friends and his self-respect.

She rose and crossed to where he stood by the window overlooking the dark street below. He sucked in an unsteady breath and her spices-and-flowers scent filled his nostrils. "How did you do it? How did you find the courage to make your own life?"

The uncertainty in her eyes knocked him senseless. If she'd boldly come on to him, whispered naughty intentions in his ear or just planted those delicious red lips on his, he could have resisted her. Probably. But the doubts clouding her eyes shredded his defenses.

"What's wrong with your life?" From where he stood, her life looked pretty damned good.

She tipped her head back. Her breath swept across his lips and his pulse stalled. "Expectations. Theirs. Mine. Sometimes it feels like my life's not my own and what I want doesn't matter."

Sympathy softened his clenched muscles. This was the stuff she hadn't told the reporter, either, the first night or tonight. And he'd bet these were the demons that had driven her to buy him at the auction. He wanted to know more and yet he didn't. Knowing meant understanding. Understanding meant weakening. Weakening meant failing. Himself. Kelly. The girls. Juliana.

He didn't want to like Juliana, didn't want to respect her,

but if anybody could understand the pressure of others' expectations, he could.

He rolled his tense shoulders. "I know what you mean. For as far back as I can remember, my life was mapped out. Most kids get asked what they want to be when they grow up. Nobody ever asked me. I was born to take over the family ranch like my father and my grandfather before him."

"But that's not what you wanted?"

Just thinking about being tied to the ranch made his skin shrink. "I didn't want to spend year after year worrying about drought, disease or whether there would be enough money left to put food on the table after a rough winter. I didn't want to die young because I worked myself into an early grave like my grandfather. I wanted more. And I wanted out. Out of that one-stoplight town. Out from under my father's thumb."

Why hadn't he ever tried to explain his fears to his parents instead of hurling abuse at them? "I took off. But not without burning my bridges first. I followed my heart. That doesn't mean it didn't get me into trouble."

Her teeth worried her bottom lip. He fisted his hands against the urge to free the soft swell from assault. "So you do understand. And all I need is the courage to follow my heart?"

"Something like that, but there are always consequences for the choices you make, Juliana. And sometimes by the time you realize the price you've paid is too high, it's too late to fix it."

All she needed was courage, but courage was the one thing Juliana lacked most at the moment.

If this had been a face-off with the top dog at the FDIC, she'd have been rock steady, but all she wanted was to feel like a woman instead of a pawn in a banking merger. The passion in Rex's kiss could give her that.

His heat and masculine scent ensnared her. Juliana's legs trembled and she felt slightly dizzy from an adrenaline rush. Couldn't he tell how much she needed his touch? Why wouldn't he kiss her?

Why don't you kiss him?

A novel idea. And a scary one. But taking an active role wasn't nearly as scary as it once had been because she liked and trusted Rex.

But what if he rebuffed her again? Would she have to give up and admit her tepid romance with Wally was all she deserved? A touch of panic quickened her pulse.

"What is it you want so badly?" he asked.

"I want to take control of my life, to do something just because I want to not because it's expected or because it's the wisest course of action." She swallowed and dampened her lips. "I want you, Rex Tanner."

His eyes slammed shut and his jaw muscles bunched. "Bad idea."

"I think it's a great idea." Faking moxie she didn't possess, she rose on tiptoe and pressed her lips to his. He stiffened and remained as rigid as a sun-baked brick wall while she brushed her lips over his once, twice, a third time. If not for the rapid hammering of his heart beneath the palms she'd braced on his chest, she'd think him unaffected. Encouraged by that telling sign, she licked his bottom lip. A groan rumbled from deep in his throat.

Slowly, she settled back on her feet. "Show me how to take control, Rex."

A battle raged in his eyes. Just when she'd convinced herself she'd played her cards and lost, and her hopes began to sink, he snatched her upper arms, yanked her close and slammed his mouth over hers in a hard, unrestrained kiss.

Shock lasted scant seconds and then a myriad of sensations

engulfed her. The inferno of his tongue as it sliced through the seam of her lips to tangle with hers, the heat of his hands as they splayed over her hips and pulled her against the branding iron of his erection combined with his taste and scent to overwhelm and arouse her beyond her wildest expectations. The infusion of pure, undiluted passion made Juliana drunk with desire and doubly glad she'd never been exposed to this level of arousal before, because without a doubt, the rush was addictive.

His hands skated upward until his thumbs reached the bare skin above her jeans. He drew circles on either side of her navel. She broke the kiss to gasp for air. The simple caress made her a lover of low-rider jeans for life. Her gaze lifted from his beard-shadowed jaw to kiss-dampened lips and then to his dark, hungry eyes.

His unblinking gaze held hers as one big hand coiled in the dangling end of her belt, holding her captive. The other raked upward, sweeping beneath her voile camisole and over her waist and ribs to cup her breast. Her fragile bra was no barrier to the back-and-forth motion of his thumb over the sensitive tip. A knot of need tightened in her belly, pulling tauter with each slow pass until every thought centered on quenching the fire he'd ignited. Her lids grew heavy. She fought to stay focused on Rex's face.

No man had ever looked at her that way, as if he would strip her bare and take her where she stood or die trying.

She liked it. Liked knowing she'd reached the limits of his control. And hers.

A shiver chased over her skin. She'd always dreamed of a man who wanted her—*her*—not the Alden heiress. And she'd found him. Too bad forever wasn't in the cards. Even if she wasn't a boring bank auditor who calculated the odds of every endeavor, she could never hold the attention of a man who thrived on taking risks, a man who had the courage to confront his fears.

But she wouldn't think about that. Not now.

He worked magic with his fingers, teasing her, tantalizing her. Her nails curled and unfurled against his chest, but his T-shirt was in the way. She wanted to touch his skin. Before she could pull the hem of his shirt from his waistband, he'd released the front catch of her bra and palmed her. Rational thought evaporated the moment his hot fingers enclosed her. She dug her nails into his waist, fisting cotton and tugging him closer.

His mouth slanted over hers, softer this time, but still ravenous. He suckled her bottom lip, bit it gently and then soothed her with his tongue.

One of them was trembling. Her? Him? Who cared?

He removed his hand, and she whimpered a protest at the loss of warmth, but then he whisked her top over her head and crushed the fragile fabric in his hand. He lifted it to his face and inhaled deeply as if drawing in her essence. Wow. So sexy. And then Rex backed toward the bedroom, leading her by the leash of her macramé belt. Her heart raced, yet her feet seemed to move in slow motion.

Inside the bedroom he stopped. "You're a smart lady. Tell me to get out."

She gulped air and responded by closing and locking the door. He dropped her blouse and flicked her bra straps over her shoulders with one finger. Juliana shrugged and the lacy garment fell to the floor. Rex traced the curves of her breasts with his eyes and then with long fingers. He grazed her tight nipples with his short nails and her breath shuddered in and out again. Dragging her by her belt, he backed toward the bed and sat, pulling her between his splayed legs to take her nipple into his hot mouth.

Her head fell back on a moan. She slapped her fingers over her mouth. With the girls next door, she had to be quiet. And for the first time in her life, being quiet during sex might be a challenge.

Rex untied her belt, but held both ends, holding her hostage—not that she intended going anywhere now that he was finally doing what she'd hoped for all along. He ravaged her breasts with gentle scrapes of his raspy evening beard, soft tugs from his seductive lips and silken swipes from his hot, wet tongue, and then he drew her deep into his mouth. Her knees wobbled. She dug her fingers into his shoulders and then tangled them in his hair. His leather tie was in the way. She pulled it free and combed her fingers through the long, soft strands.

Rex plucked at the button and zip of her jeans. His knuckles brushed her navel and her stomach muscles rippled involuntarily. His big palm scorched a path from one hip to the other as he eased the snug denim down one inch at a time. By the time he got the fabric to her knees, she was ready to rip her jeans off, throw them across the room and beg him to fill the empty ache expanding inside her. She braced herself on his shoulders and stepped out of the pants. Eager, impatient, she burned with an unfamiliar urgency.

Rex drew back to examine her itty-bitty panties with an appreciative gaze. Had she ever felt this desirable in her life? No. *Bless the lingerie store at the mall.*

His fingers hooked under the lace, raking her panties down her legs and discarding them, and then he lifted her jeans from the floor, pulled the belt free of the loops and stretched it between his hands. With slow, deliberate movements he wound the ends around each wrist. Her heart missed a beat.

"Close your eyes and turn around, Juliana." The rough order made her quiver.

The time for her walk on the wild side had arrived. The question was did she have the courage to follow through?

Seven

Last chance. Last chance.

With her pulse thumping a deafening beat in her ears, Juliana lowered her lids and turned her back to Rex. The air around her stirred, sweeping over her skin as Rex shifted behind her. A second later, something alternately cool and rough crossed her breasts. Startled, she peeked. Her belt.

He dragged the braided strands left, right and back again and again. Each of the glass beads woven into the pattern teased her like a cool fingertip, while the cording, similar to the mild calluses on Rex's palms, lightly abraded her skin. The heat of his breath between her shoulder blades was her only warning before he nuzzled her hair aside and placed an open-mouthed kiss on her nape followed by another on her neck and her shoulder, her back…

Nipping. Kissing. Grazing.

His teeth. His lips. The belt.

She thought she'd implode as each new sensation built upon the last. A shudder shook her.

The belt slid lower, gliding over her waist, hips and curls. She gasped as the beads bumped over her highly sensitized flesh. And then he took the belt on a return trip, raking her nerve endings into a combustible pile and turning her legs to rubber.

"Turn around."

She forced her uncooperative muscles into obedience. The belt tightened beneath the curve of her bottom. Her nails bit into her palms and her teeth clenched on a moan as the beaded strands slid to her calves, ankles and back again. Rex pulled her closer. She braced her hands on his chest and then lowered them to his belly and bunched his T-shirt in her hands. She had to feel his skin on hers.

This couldn't possibly get better. Could it? She had to find out. She tugged upward and opened her eyes, reveling in the hunger she found in his. "Rex, please, I need to feel you against me."

He pitched the belt onto the bed behind him and helped her remove his shirt. She flexed her fingers, anticipating touching him. And then she did, burying her fingers in the dark curls on his chest, but reality far exceeded fantasy. Supple hot satin rippled below her fingertips. The tickle of his wiry hairs teased her palms. And then she cupped his face and kissed him. She couldn't possibly find the words to express how good he made her feel, but she could show him by pouring it into her kiss.

Rex's arms banded around her, fusing her to the length of his hot torso as he consumed her mouth roughly, greedily. It wasn't enough. Juliana wanted more, needed more, ached for more. As if he read her thoughts, he shifted her until she strad- dled one muscled thigh. The position left her open and vul- nerable, a situation he took advantage of by easing his fingers between them to comb through her curls, find her wetness and caress her with deft strokes until she weaved unsteadily on her trembling legs. He pressed deeper, stroked faster and the tension inside her twisted into an almost unbearable knot.

She broke the kiss to gulp for air and alternately tangled her fingers in his hair and clenched his shoulders. His bristly jaw abraded the tender underside of her breast and then he caught her nipple with his lips, his teeth and gently tormented her right over the edge of reason. Release arced through her, scattering sparks clear down to her toes.

She forced her heavy lids open and smiled into his dark eyes. She traced a finger over his tight jaw. "Wow."

"Condoms. Get 'em," he rasped.

She turned to do as he bid, opening the purse she'd left on the dresser and retrieving the box with trembling hands. By the time she turned around he'd removed his boots and socks and stood towering over her. Juliana's heart pounded out a nervous rhythm as he shed his jeans and briefs with one sharp shove. His hair was wild and disheveled from her handiwork, and he looked every inch the rebel with the stubble on his jaw and upper lip and an untamed look in his eyes.

Her gaze skated over his broad chest to the erection jutting from a bed of dense dark curls. Thick. Hard. Hers. At least for now. Her mouth dried and her pulse blipped hummingbird fast.

Rex wanted her. *Her.* His desire was there plain to see. No man had ever been so blatantly aroused by just pleasuring her. In fact, few had ever taken the time to make sure she enjoyed the encounter.

He ripped back the comforter and held out his hand. She laid hers in his big palm and he drew her closer. The impact of his hot arousal against her belly sent her breath shuddering from her lungs and then his mouth took hers in a deep, soul-robbing kiss. The condoms fell from her fingers as she gave in to her need to stroke his supple skin, test his thick muscles and cup the derriere she'd shamelessly ogled when no one was looking.

He tipped her toward the mattress. The cool glide of his hair over her shoulder and then her breast had to be the most sensual thing Juliana had ever experienced. No wonder so many men liked long hair. Rex's dragged like cool satin over her heated skin as he feasted on her breasts, her belly. His tongue dipped into her navel and then swirled a path from hip bone to hip bone. It was simultaneously too much and not enough.

When he *finally* parted her curls and found her with his mouth, she had to shove her fist against her mouth to quiet her cries. She'd wanted to experience passion, and boy, was she. All too quickly, release undulated through her. Never had she felt anything this intense and at the same time frightening. Frightening because she was out of control, a slave to her desires, and because she had a feeling Rex Tanner was more man that she—or any woman for that matter—could handle. He'd be a rocket ride to heartbreak for any woman foolish enough to expect more than short-term thrills.

Good thing that temporary was all she wanted.

Wasn't it?

Doubts nipped at her conscience. Could she be happy with *nice* after this?

The self-indulgent beast rode Rex's back, clawing for sexual satisfaction the way it used to after a concert—only worse. The fangs of need sank deeper into his flesh than ever before.

Give, you selfish SOB. For once in your life give. Don't take.

He fought to leash his raging hunger and let Juliana drag him up her body one excruciating inch at a time, and then he grabbed the discarded box of condoms and shoved it in her hand. His entire body quaked with the effort it took to restrain himself from taking her—using her—to slake his hunger.

"You want control? Take it." His voice came out raspy and rough, as if he'd played in too many gigs in smoke-filled bars.

Surprise flashed in Juliana's passion-glazed eyes. Her breasts jiggled as her breath shuddered in and then out again, fueling his desire. He cradled her, marveling in the softness of the pale skin filling his palms and the sexy little sounds she made when he rolled her nipples between his fingers and thumbs. Those whimpers almost did him in.

Her hands trembled as she carefully slid a fingernail beneath the flap, opened the box and selected a condom. He'd given her the task because he wanted her so badly he was beyond finesse. He'd have shredded the damned box like an overly enthusiastic teen. Juliana gently tore the plastic wrapper with her fingers. He'd have ripped it open with his teeth. And then she slowly and carefully withdrew the protection.

He'd bet she was the kind who never tore wrapping paper. If he weren't about to burst out of his skin, he might have appreciated her diligence and savored the anticipation of having her hands on him, but right now he was too busy losing his mind to appreciate anything. Fisting his hands, he braced himself, but nothing could prepare him for her light, delicate touch as she smoothed the latex over him.

He ground his teeth and concentrated on a complicated riff. The soft, downward sweep of her fingers came close to stopping his heart and melting his brain, and then her fingers tightened around him. She stroked him from base to tip once, twice, a third time. Too good. Too intense. But he'd promised her control and, dammit, he'd let her have it if it killed him. Which it just might. His breath whistled in through gritted teeth, and he shook with the effort to hold on, but he couldn't stop the groan boiling from his chest.

The glow of feminine power radiated from her blue eyes, darkened her cheekbones and curved her damp red lips. She knelt over him, straddling his thighs, and he prayed she'd put him out of his misery. The faster the better.

She reached over his shoulder for her belt and his pulse stuttered. *Bondage?* The banker didn't seem the type. Not that he couldn't learn to like sex games if this affair continued. Which it shouldn't. Couldn't.

Wouldn't.

He couldn't bring her down to his sewer-rat level.

But instead of winding the belt around his wrists, she trailed the knotted ends across his chest and then over his belly like a dozen caressing fingers. The cool beads swept over his skin, electrifying him like a shorted-out microphone. She snaked the belt around his erection and slowly slithered it free. Holy spit. She *would* kill him. He bowed off the bed, pitching her forward until her soft breasts seared his chest. Fisting his hand in her hair, he drew her mouth to his and kissed her until his lungs burned.

"Stop torturing me," he warned against her mouth.

He felt her smile against his lips, and then she drew back a few inches and he saw laughter in her eyes. He teetered closer to the edge of reason. "Am I torturing you?"

"You know it." He grasped her hips and dragged her forward until her hot, wet body covered his, urging her to take him where he needed to be—inside. But she didn't. She rocked, sliding slick and hot along his length and ripping a hoarse groan straight from his gut. He fisted his hands in the sheet. Wild and impatient, the selfish demon inside him roared. He could give into the clawing hunger and become the self-absorbed SOB who used women or fight it and let Juliana have her way.

He'd fight. But *damn,* it was hard.

And then he decided two could play this seductive torment-ing game. He raked his palms up Juliana's thighs, found her moisture with his fingers and plied her sensitive flesh until her back arched and she writhed with pleasure. Her gaze locked with his and his heart slammed against his chest.

Take her. Take her. Do it. Now.

She splayed her fingers over his chest and paused with him poised at heaven's gate. His muscles bunched. He was a split second away from tossing her on her back, ramming home and selfishly taking his pleasure, when Juliana took him with a slow slide deep into the blistering, wet glove of her body.

His lungs emptied in a rush. Stars flashed behind his eyelids. He forced his eyes open and the pleasure magnified. He'd never seen a more seductive sight than Juliana riding him. With her skin flushed and her swollen lips parted, she gasped for breath and then she opened her eyes and met his gaze with a blaze of white-hot passion. Never mind that every deliberate swivel of her hips destroyed dozens of his brain cells, he liked seeing her this way, liked watching Juliana come unglued.

He stroked her, pushing her toward another release, and then her breath hitched and she clenched him tight. Rex lost it. He grasped her waist and held her as he thrust deep and hard and fast as one explosion after another detonated in his body, rocking him with pleasure more intense than any he'd ever experienced.

Juliana collapsed against him and his arms encircled her automatically as if they'd done that before. They hadn't. He'd never held a woman after he'd used her. But he wanted to hold Juliana, wanted to keep her close.

Trouble. Damn, he was in trouble.

He stared at the ceiling in numb silence as Juliana slipped off him and into the crook of his shoulder. His heart slowed, but his muscles didn't relax. He couldn't get a word past the anger and self-disgust choking him as Juliana curled her fingers on his chest. Moments later, her body went slack as sleep took her. She wouldn't rest as easily and she sure as hell wouldn't be wearing that satisfied smile if she knew what kind of man she'd shared her body with.

He was clean, disease free. He made damned sure of that by getting tested often. But Juliana deserved better than him. Hell, any woman deserved better than a guy who couldn't remember the names or faces of more than a handful of his past lovers.

It had been so easy to believe the hype and the media, too easy to believe the world owed him and not the other way around. He'd taken the female fans who'd wanted to show their appreciation in a sexual way as his due. Physical release had been his drug of choice, and now that he had a hit of pure ecstasy coursing through his veins, he wasn't sure he'd be able to resist the lure again.

He didn't know how to have a healthy sexual relationship. Sure, he'd tried a few times, but monogamy hadn't worked. He'd never stuck with one woman long because he couldn't. He lacked the gene or the moral fiber or whatever it was that made a man capable of committing. He was flawed.

Loving Juliana—no, not loving—*sex* with Juliana had unleashed the beast that used women, the jackass who'd disgraced his family and himself.

His parents had never attended his concerts. The demands of the ranch had made getting away for a weekend almost impossible. Then one night, his family had surprised him after a big show. Rex hadn't known they were there until the roadie had opened the dressing-room door to show them in.

His mother, father and sister had stopped in horrified silence on the threshold, their wide eyes going from Rex to the half-naked groupie coiled around him. Rex had quickly zipped his pants and tucked in his shirttails. But the damage had been done.

Hell, he'd been inside the woman, but he hadn't known her name and couldn't introduce her to his family. He'd watched realization dawn on his mother's face quickly followed by embarrassment and shame. He'd turned to his father, expecting a guy to understand—boys will be boys and all that—but he'd seen disappointment and disgust. And then he'd looked at Kelly's flushed face. The pride he'd always seen in his sister's big brown eyes hadn't been there.

Rex hadn't been raised that way. He'd been taught since he was knee-high to respect others—especially women. And here he was doing the opposite. Using. Discarding. He'd never forget the awkward tension filling the room as the groupie had straightened her clothing, collected an autograph—because they never left without one—and then she'd squeezed out the door. His family had left right behind her without saying a word.

One sad, disapproving glance over his mother's shoulder had said it all. Rex had become a man not even a mother could love.

He'd been ashamed of his behavior. But had he learned his lesson? No, he'd defiantly kept right on carousing right up until the day his parents had died.

Self-disgust rolled over him. Tonight he'd begun the cycle of self-destruction again. Without a doubt, he'd made a mistake in getting physical with Juliana Alden.

The question was could he undo the damage?

Or was it too late?

Juliana awoke to limbs weighted with satisfaction, a smile she couldn't suppress and an empty bed. The latter niggled like an account entry that didn't belong, but she brushed aside her misgivings. Last night had been amazing. Rex was the most unselfish lover she'd ever had, and he'd brought out a sensual side of her that she hadn't known existed.

How had she made it to the age of thirty without experiencing such wonderful, levitating, delectable passion? Had to be the man. Self-service orgasms and the partners from her past just couldn't measure up to Rex Tanner. But then he reportedly had a lot of experience pleasing women.

She cast off the strangely disturbing thought and glanced at the bedside clock. It was far too early for Rex or the girls to be up, but late enough that Juliana should consider getting ready for work soon. She didn't want to. For the first time ever, she wanted to call in sick so she and Rex could replay last night's passionate encounter.

Passionate. Her. Yes, *her*. Bubbles of anticipation floated through her bloodstream. Reality quickly and brutally popped them. This was only lust, wasn't it? She wouldn't have slept with Rex if she hadn't liked him, but she'd never intended their month together to be more than a last fling and an opportunity to prove to Andrea and Holly that she wasn't missing out on anything by following her mother's suggestion to marry Wally.

No, this heady feeling couldn't be more than lust. She wasn't an impulsive person, and she never made important decisions without thoroughly researching her options. Logic always triumphed over emotion, and logic said Wally was proper husband material. She couldn't afford to fall for Rex, so she wouldn't. It was as simple as that. She had two and a half weeks to enjoy his company, and then she'd fulfill her obligations.

Last chance. Last chance.

The straitjacket of expectations tightened around her, making it difficult to take a breath. Goose bumps rose on her skin and her stomach churned. Swallowing her rising anxiety, Juliana sat up and shoved her hair off her face with an unsteady hand. The ceiling fan overhead whirled, cooling her naked skin. She could handle a purely physical relationship. Couldn't she?

Certainly. Other women did it all the time.

Rising from the bed, she listened for Rex in the adjoining bathroom, but heard nothing. Where could he be? And then she caught sight of her face in the mirror over his dresser and grimaced. Her hair looked like she'd been through a hurricane, and she had mascara smudges beneath her eyes. Vanity forced her to take a quick shower, brush her teeth and apply a touch of makeup. She combed her damp hair, shrugged into her bathrobe and then eased open the bedroom door and jerked to a halt.

Déjà vu. Rex slept on the sofa, wearing only unbuttoned jeans. Her smile faded and a sinking feeling settled in the pit of her stomach. Why would he sleep out here when he had a perfectly good bed—and her—in his room?

Doubt crept over her like an incoming fog. Hadn't he enjoyed last night as much as she had? Her achy well-loved muscles and the love bites and beard burn he'd left on her skin indicated he had. But maybe she hadn't measured up to Rex's other lovers.

Horrified, she pressed a hand to her chest. Had he been faking it? With her vast experience at faking it, surely she would have recognized pretense?

Maybe he was trying to shelter the girls from the adult side of his and Juliana's relationship. She liked that idea better than thinking he might prefer the too-short sofa to sleeping with her.

Part of her wanted to shake him awake and pepper him with questions until she had her answers. Her more cautious side feared what she'd hear. Confrontation wasn't a problem for her at work where she knew her subject and often had the supporting data in front of her, but in her personal life, she sucked at it and this morning… She bit her lip and tightened the belt of her robe. Why wasn't there a manual for mornings after?

She tiptoed into the kitchen and flipped the switch on the coffeepot. Within seconds, the appliance gurgled to life. Juliana watched Rex, half hoping the machine's noisy hisses and coughs would rouse him. From where she stood, she could see the top of his head, his shoulders and chest. The sudden change in the cadence of his breathing made her pulse quicken. In moments, she'd have her answers. Like them or not.

Rex lifted his left wrist, checking his watch, she guessed, and then he swiped his hand over his face. She wished she could see his expression. Was he smiling as she'd been when she'd first awakened? Or did he have regrets?

He inhaled deeply, and then sat up and shoved his hair back with both hands. His head turned abruptly and he spotted her. She saw the exact second he recalled the intimacy they'd shared. Tension stiffened his features and his spine straightened. Not a good sign when she'd hoped for a smile and a hello-babe-let's-go-back-to-bed-before-the-girls-awake kiss.

Clinging to his earlier declaration that he wasn't a morning person and hoping that was the only cause of his less than happy-to-see-her reaction, Juliana swallowed to ease the dryness in her mouth. "Good morning."

"'Morning." He slowly rose and faced her with a dark, inscrutable gaze.

The blatant masculinity in his beard-roughened face, broad chest and the unbuttoned jeans sent adrenaline and estrogen pulsing through her system. "You didn't have to sleep out here."

"Yeah, I did."

"Because you didn't want the girls to find us in bed together?" If she were a superstitious person, she'd cross her fingers.

"Because last night shouldn't have happened. It won't happen again."

The arousal simmering in her stomach turned cold and hard like cooling candle wax. Last night she'd had the best sex of her life and he was willing to dismiss it? "I'm sorry to hear that. Do you mind if I ask why?"

"Yes."

She waited for him to elaborate. When he didn't, she asked, "Yes what?"

"Yes, I mind if you ask."

"That was a rhetorical question. Why can't we make love again?"

A nerve in his jaw twitched. "Look, Juliana, you're an attractive woman. It's been a while since I... It's been a while for me. I should have controlled myself last night."

This grew worse by the second. "Are you saying you were just scratching an itch and any woman would have done?"

He hesitated and those silent seconds crushed her heart in a vise. Breathless with pain, Juliana turned back to the coffeepot and filled a mug with unsteady hands. She didn't want the fragrant brew, didn't even know if she could keep it in her churning stomach, but she couldn't face him right now.

And then an even more painful realization hit. Lust wouldn't hurt this much. That meant that her feelings for Rex might be more than simple physical desire. Was she falling for him? Her heart pounded. No, she couldn't be. He didn't fit in with her life plan or her career goals.

"Juliana, I'm sorry."

She straightened her spine, lifted her chin and met his solemn gaze. She tightened her fingers around the mug in a grip that would break more fragile china. "I'm not sorry."

She wasn't. Taking control of their relationship, her sexual pleasure and her life was—what had he said?—oh, yes, a journey she had to take. But she wasn't the auditor with the highest success rate at Alden Bank and Trust for nothing. When she wanted something, she didn't give up without a fight. And she wanted more of the passion Rex Tanner had shown her. More of her reluctant rebel. She wanted—needed—to store up memories for later.

Did he want the same? She didn't know, but she'd learned early on that if you wanted something and didn't speak up, then you got exactly what you asked for. Nothing. And if that meant she had to become the seducer instead of the seducee then she'd willingly take on the role.

Rex exhaled harshly. "You don't get it. I can't be the man you need. You're hearts and flowers and forever. I'm not. I let people down, Juliana. It's what I do best."

Forever? Her mind snagged on the word. "I didn't ask for forever, Rex. All I'm asking for are the two and a half weeks remaining in your auction package."

His jaw muscles bunched.

She closed the gap between them and opened her hand over his chest. His heart beat frantically beneath her palm. "Seventeen days, Rex. That's all I want."

Now that you've tasted passion, can you live without it?

Of course she could. She had her life mapped out and if she wanted to make it to the top, the way her mother had, then Juliana couldn't afford detours. Especially not the kind that made her think of taking days off to laze in bed with a lover.

Eight

Apparently his momma had raised a fool, Rex told himself as he stopped outside his open bedroom door.

Otherwise Juliana's offer of a no-strings-attached relationship wouldn't have his mouth salivating and his heart palpitating at the sight of her lying on his bed in a puddle of moonlight and tangled sheets. Obviously he'd learned nothing from his past.

He wanted her as badly as he wanted his next breath. If her alarm hadn't sounded this morning immediately after she'd dropped her offer on the table, then—right or wrong—he probably would have dragged her back to bed, shoved her robe from her shoulders and buried himself deep inside her.

Forget the bed. He would have taken her in the kitchen. He'd been that hot, that eager, and it hadn't taken giving a performance in front of tens of thousands of screaming fans to get him harder than a steel rod. Juliana had managed that feat all by herself, which meant she had the power to take him lower than he'd been when he'd hit rock bottom. Not good.

But damn, he craved her. Craved her like an addict needing a fix.

Quit thinking with your balls, Tanner.

His eyes adjusted to the darkness of the apartment. In the silence at two in the morning, he could hear the whisper of Juliana's breath. She lay on her side with her dark hair spread across his pillow just the way she'd been last night when he'd forced himself to leave her.

His heart thumped hard and fast, like a beater against a bass drum in an up-tempo song.

Head for the sofa. But his feet didn't move and his unblinking gaze remained fixed on the woman who'd dominated his thoughts all day. The ceiling fan stirred the air, surrounding him in her scent.

Accepting her offer isn't the same as using her.

Wasn't it? Would he be backsliding into that selfish SOB mindset if he gave her what she wanted? Hell, he'd never intended to live the rest of his life like a monk.

If not celibacy, then what do you have planned, bucko?

Nothing. The answer surprised him. All his life, he'd worked toward a goal. First on getting off the ranch, second, on landing a record contract, and then on making it to the top of the charts. He'd accomplished all three, leaving a trail of casualties in his selfish, self-destructive wake. After his parents' deaths, he'd set his sights on getting out of Nashville. Once he'd managed that, he'd focused on getting Renegade open and making himself available to Kelly and the girls. Once again, mission accomplished, but this time he had no intention of hurting or disappointing anyone.

His personal life hadn't figured anywhere in the equation.

Now what? He pinched his knotted neck muscles. If one-night stands were out of the question, then was he looking for something more? Something permanent? Was he marriage material? Probably not. But maybe after he had the bank note paid off, he could be for someone willing to take a chance on a rough-off-the-ranch guy who was trying to get his priorities straight. Someone strong enough to yank him back in line when he tried to take what he wanted without giving back.

Someone like Juliana.

Whoa. Back up.

As much as he liked and desired Juliana and appreciated her stepping in to help out with the girls, he couldn't see the banking heiress settling for an almost broke high-school dropout who'd burned all his bridges. Even if she did want him, her dragon lady of a mother wouldn't accept him into the family, and he refused to come between Juliana and her folks. One of these days, she'd realize what he cost her, and she'd hate him for it the way he hated himself for letting his selfishness ruin his relationship with his family.

But a relationship—even a temporary one—with Juliana wouldn't be another nameless, faceless encounter like the ones from his past, the devil's advocate in his head argued. He not only knew her name and where she lived, he knew her favorite flavor of ice cream—peach—and a dozen other details about her, like her cautious nature, the way she weighed the risks before making a move, the sarcasm that sneaked out when she was nervous and her tendency to research everything from him to motorcycle manuals to child care. As for her face, he'd never forget it.

Go for it.

He took a step toward the bed, but stopped. Juliana had not only resurrected his libido, she'd made him think about music, and that scared the hell out of him. He'd had that damned song—the one he'd been writing the day his parents had died—in his head all day. Music had been his salvation once, but it had also become his damnation, his path to ruin. He couldn't let music back into his life. Too risky.

Juliana shifted, rolled on to her back. "Rex, is that you?"

He swallowed. "Yeah."

She threw back the sheet and sat up. Moonlight danced over her bare skin. "Lock the door and come to bed."

His fists clenched and his chest burned. He sucked in a forgotten breath.

What the hell. You're damned anyway.

His fingers turned the lock and his feet carried him forward. He stopped beside the mattress and prayed for the strength to turn around before it was too late. And then Juliana rose on her knees, and any chance he had of saving his damned soul vanished when her cheek pressed his chest over his hammering heart.

He peeled his shirt over his head and joined her in the bed. And he hoped like hell he wouldn't hate himself more than he already did in the morning.

Juliana looked across the sun-dappled playground to where Rex crouched beside Becky and Liza in the sandbox and saw something she hadn't even known she'd missed.

Neither of her parents would have played hooky from work to waste a day building sand castles that afternoon storms would wash away or let their little girl cup their face with sandy hands to plant sticky kisses on their cheeks the way Liza did to Rex. In Juliana's world, hugs had been allowed only when she was neat and tidy. Irma had dealt with the messy side of life, the sticky kisses, the dirty hands, the skinned knees and the difficult questions of a teenage girl trying to understand her changing body and the rascally boys at school.

A few yards from Rex and the girls, a woman blew bubbles.

Her children chased them, squealing and laughing and falling down to roll in the sand. At a picnic table farther down the park, a gathering of preschoolers and their mothers celebrated a birthday with songs and games. The joy on all those faces, young and old, opened an aching void in Juliana's chest. If she followed in her mother's footsteps, would she ever have moments like these?

Liza's laughter drew Juliana's gaze back to the sandbox. Rex lifted his head and their gazes met. He spoke to the girls, and then rose and stalked toward her, wearing a sexy, melt-her-bones smile. He could make her heart pound with nothing more than a look. Did she have a similar effect on him? If so, he concealed it well. Not that he hadn't been an amazing and generous lover the past two nights, but she had a feeling she was the only one losing control in bed. Her work had taught her to recognize the signs when someone was concealing information. Rex was holding something back and she wanted to know what.

The T-shirt he'd pulled on over his swim trunks after climbing from the pool hugged his powerful chest. An afternoon breeze fluttered the hem over his flat stomach. Her gaze skimmed down to his hairy legs. Her palms tingled. She adored the rough texture of his legs against her skin when they made love, and making love with Rex… Warmth washed over her. Suffice to say she'd never doubt her capacity for passion again.

"Glad you took the day off?" Rex sat down beside her on the picnic-table bench, straddling the wood so he faced her with his splayed knees bracketing her. One of his big hands swept up and down her spine and the other landed on her thigh beneath the picnic table.

"Yes." And more than a little surprised. Shirking work wasn't like her. Her pulse skipped erratically as Rex's long, lightly calloused fingers inched beneath the hem of her shorts to trace the elastic leg opening of her panties. She glanced around quickly, but no one could see his mischief beneath the table. Arousal coiled hot and low in her belly, shortening her breath and moistening her mouth.

He played her body as well as he played his guitar on the CDs she and the girls secretly listened to in the car. Juliana struggled against her thought-numbing response. She'd never understand what made Rex tick if she kept letting him distract her. "What did you mean when you said you let people down?"

Rex's spine stiffened and his smile faded. He removed his hands and turned on the bench to face the girls. Instantly, Juliana missed the warmth of his touch.

"I meant I let people down."

"Yes, I got that part. But who? How?"

He exhaled heavily. "Juliana—"

His none-of-your-business tone told her he was going to brush aside her curiosity again the way he'd done each time she'd asked personal questions. She didn't intend to let him avoid answering this time.

"Please, Rex, I've read so much conflicting information about you online that I'd like to know the truth."

Silent seconds ticked past. The girls giggled and added another leaning tower to their sand castle. Birds chirped. None of the other park visitors seemed to be sharing her knife-edge of tension.

"I already told you that I hated the ranch." He hesitated, bracing his elbows on his knees and lacing his fingers. To anyone else, he probably looked relaxed, but Juliana saw the whiteness of his knuckles. "What I didn't tell you was that my folks tried to talk me out of going to Nashville. They didn't want me to chase a dream that was more likely to die than come true. Their intentions were good. They didn't want me to be hurt. But I didn't see it that way. Before I left, I said some obnoxious stuff to them about being ignorant hayseeds who had no ambition to better themselves."

"How old were you?"

"Eighteen."

"You were just a kid. Everybody knows kids—especially teens—aren't known for making the wisest choices." Except for her. She'd always done the right thing for fear of the consequences.

His head swiveled toward her. "I was old enough to know better. I should have shown more respect. But I didn't. I really let 'er rip. I can't remember half of the garbage I spewed."

"Should I quote the cliché about hindsight being clearer?"

He stared at the girls and his Adam's apple bobbed as he swallowed. "I had a couple of rough years in Nashville. Mom sent money I knew they couldn't spare. I didn't ask for it, but I took it. I was broke enough to humble myself that much, but not enough to apologize. I *never* apologized. Dad wrote and told me I could come home. I told him I'd live in the streets first."

The pain and regret in his voice made her heart ache. Juliana curled her fingers around the tensed muscles of his biceps and squeezed in a silent show of support.

"When I was twenty-two I lucked out. I was hanging out in a seedy bar. I couldn't even afford a beer, so I just sat in a back corner and listened to the music. The singer onstage was pretty bad. The crowd got rowdy. Somebody threw a beer bottle at him. It caught the guy upside the head and knocked him out. It looked like hell was gonna break loose and I was a long way from the exit. So I went the other way. I climbed on the stage, grabbed the man's guitar and started belting out songs as hard and fast as I could, hoping to head off something ugly while his bandmates tried to revive him. The crowd settled. The singer came to. I got off the stage and headed for the door. A guy from the audience followed me and offered me a record deal right there on Second Avenue. Turns out he was a bigwig at one of the labels. And the rest…" He shrugged.

"The rest is history. But I want to hear the part I can't read on the Internet. Who did you let down and how?"

"You ever let folks down?" His dark gaze pinned her to the bench.

Only recently, but she hoped her mother would get over Juliana buying Rex. "I've always been the rule-following type. I toed the line because I was paralyzed by the idea of disappointing my parents."

"Thought so."

That stung. But she didn't want to talk about her cowardice or the difficult conversations that lay ahead, because it had taken her thirty years to find the nerve that Rex had possessed at eighteen. "I admire your courage in following your dreams. What happened after the record deal?"

"I started making money. I sent some home. I guess I wanted to make amends for being a jackass, but I couldn't swallow my pride enough to show up and apologize in person. Hell, I didn't even have the guts to call and say it over the phone.

"And then it was too late. A couple of years ago, Mom and Dad were killed in a tornado. I never thanked them for supporting me. And I never said I'm sorry. They died thinking their son was an ungrateful, selfish son of a bitch. And they were right."

Juliana slid her arm around his waist. "I don't think you're selfish."

"That's because you don't know me. I had a concert scheduled the day of the funeral. Would you believe I actually had to stop and think about where I wanted to be? Where I *ought* to be? In the end, I asked Kelly to reschedule the funeral for an earlier time and then I chartered a private jet so I could do both—the funeral and later, the concert. I went onstage that night and performed like nothing had happened. Like I hadn't just laid my parents in the ground.

"The next morning, I looked in the mirror and I realized I didn't like the man I'd become. I tried to get out of my contracts, but they were airtight. So I self-destructed, once again thinking about my sorry ass instead of the sixty-three people in my band and road crew who depended on me for a living."

"You were grieving, Rex, and some people deal with grief by ignoring it until they have a little distance."

He shot to his feet and looked down on her with tormented eyes. "Don't try to turn me into one of the good guys, Juliana. I'm not the man for you. What we have is good *for now*, but I won't be around for the long haul. Don't count on me."

And then he pivoted on his heel and returned to the girls. Juliana pressed a hand over the ache consuming her chest. Her heart was breaking not for herself, but for Rex.

She was no Beauty, but there was no doubt in her mind that Rex was a wounded Beast who needed someone to show him that he wasn't a monster.

That someone was her.

"Rex, visitor for you," Danny called out on Saturday afternoon.

Rex set the spreadsheets on his desk in the Renegade office and swore. Probably another customer wanting to needle him about the newspaper article. Octavia Jenkins's second installment had appeared in the paper this morning. She'd spouted more of the same fairy-tale nonsense, this time comparing his and Juliana's relationship to the Disney movie the girls had been watching on TV during Octavia's last interview.

He rose and made his way out front. Before Juliana had left for work yesterday, she'd offered—no, she'd insisted—on taking a look at his books to see if she could come up with any ideas for increasing his revenues and decreasing his overhead. He wasn't crazy about letting her see the gravity of his financial situation, but numbers were her thing. She had the fancy degree and credentials to prove it. All he had were scars from the school of hard knocks.

He glanced over the thinning lunch crowd before following Danny's pointing finger to the man sitting at the far end of the bar. Rex's muscles locked.

"Long time no see, Rex. What's up?" his former manager called out.

Rex ignored John Lee's outstretched hand. "How'd you find me?"

"What happened to 'Hello, John Lee, great to see you after all this time?'" When Rex didn't respond he continued, "My clipping service picked up that piece on you and the bachelor auction. Had to come and see for myself if it was really you. The long hair…now that's a good look on you."

Damn. Rex had known the risk of discovery going into the auction, but he'd figured after the way he'd left Nashville nobody would be interested in looking him up. "What do you want, John Lee?"

"You. You left before the label or the fans got tired of you. I read about your bar and your publicity efforts for the place. I know of a better way to draw a crowd. Say the word and I'll have a contract in front of you before happy hour starts."

"Not interested. I'd rather lose Renegade than go back to that life."

In the blink of an eye, John Lee dropped his good ol' boy facade and the sharp-as-a-new-scalpel businessman who'd taken Rex to the top of the charts took its place. "Look, Tanner, you can't walk away when you're still at the top."

Rex ground his teeth. "Newsflash. I already did."

"I know you gotta miss the women."

Strangely, Rex didn't. God knows he'd had his share of come-ons from bar patrons, but none had tempted him. Until Juliana. But his weakness with her was a sign that he wasn't cured of his addiction. "Nope."

John Lee smoothed a hand over his hundred-dollar haircut. "I know I rode you hard after your parents passed, but I was trying to help you keep your mind off their deaths. Now you've had time to get over it. C'mon back. Let's make music and money, son."

"No, thanks." He turned and strode toward his office.

"You owe a lot of folks, Rex."

The words stopped Rex cold. He slowly pivoted. "I don't owe anybody. I cleared my debts."

"What about your band? They were counting on you for another ten-year ride."

"I found jobs for every one of the guys and the roadies, too."

"But not with a headliner raking in your kind of dough. There's only one Rex Tanner."

"Yeah. And he runs a bar and grill. Have a safe trip home, John Lee."

"I'll be down the street at the Hilton for a couple of days. Think over my offer. Call me when you see the light. Cell number's the same, but here it is in case you misplaced it." He pulled a business card from the pocket of his custom-tailored western suit and offered it to Rex. Rex ignored it. John Lee laid it on the bar and then headed out the door.

Rex snatched up the card and crushed it in his fist, and then he stalked back into his office and dropped into his chair. He pitched the crumpled card on his desk. It landed on the spread-sheets. His gaze dropped to the bottom line and his gut knotted. Without a doubt he needed cash. The auction had increased business, but not enough. Unless a miracle happened, then Rex would very likely default on his loan in another forty-five days.

He missed music. No doubt about it. But could he live with himself if he accepted John Lee's offer? Rex had learned the hard way that the money's not worth jack if you can't live with the decisions you're making.

But if you were headlining again then you could afford to give Juliana the kinds of things she deserves.

Whoa. That thought blindsided him. Did he want more than great sex and a short-term affair with Juliana? He rubbed his jaw. Maybe. He'd never had a more responsive lover. God knows she lit up his light bar like nobody else ever had. He liked her, liked her cautious nature, her sarcasm, her generosity and her damned-near insatiable curiosity. She'd weaseled stuff out of him that nobody else had and done it so smoothly that he hadn't even realized what she was doing until he'd spewed his guts out.

Each day he spent with her and the girls made him wonder what it would be like to have a family. With someone like Juliana, who gave as good as she got.

He scrubbed a hand across the back of his neck. He couldn't support a family on Renegade's current earnings. If he were headlining again he could, but then Juliana wouldn't want anything to do with the kind of louse he'd become. He didn't think for one second that he was strong enough to keep the selfish monster inside him under control. Look how quickly he'd caved with Juliana.

But he had to admit, he was tempted to try. Tempted for Juliana's sake. But if he let her down, he wouldn't be able to live with himself.

A no-win situation.

And happiness… Hell, he didn't deserve it.

A noise jolted Juliana from a deep sleep. She pried open her eyes and listened. Heat blanketed her back from shoulders to knees and a heavy arm draped across her waist. She turned her head on the pillow. Rex hadn't woken her tonight.

Before she could decide what that meant, another whimper made her jerk upright. The sound came from the girls' room. She jumped from the bed and tugged on her robe.

"What's wrong?" Rex's husky whisper called through the darkness.

"One of the girls is upset." She wanted to ask him why he hadn't made love to her when he'd come to bed tonight, the way he had each night since they'd become lovers, but the cries from the other room grew louder. She dashed into the hall and then into the girls' room. Becky sobbed into her pillow.

Juliana sat on the bed, brushed back Becky's dark hair and whispered, "Bad dream?"

"Daddy," Becky wailed. "I want my daddy."

Juliana felt Rex behind her before she heard him. Heat radiated off his bare chest, drawing her like a magnet. "Remember what Mom said when she called earlier? They'll be here in the morning, Beck."

But Becky wouldn't be consoled. Rex reached past Juliana and scooped his niece into his arms. He headed for the den, but not fast enough. Liza sat up. "Whassa matter?"

Juliana kissed her brow. "Becky had a bad dream. She's okay. Go back to sleep."

"Me up, too." Liza lifted her arms. Juliana couldn't resist. She carried Liza into the darkened den and sat down on the opposite end of the sofa from Rex and Becky.

"Mommy said Daddy was h-hurt really, really b-bad and that he almost went to h-heaven," Becky choked out between sobs. "Is he...okay?"

Rex tucked her head beneath his chin and nuzzled a kiss into her hair. "He got banged up, but the doctors have fixed him. He might be slow as a snail for a while, and he'll probably need your help with some stuff, but he'll be okay. I know he's going to be happy to see his girls."

"Will he have to go back to that bad place?"

Sympathy squeezed the air from Juliana's lungs. She had no idea how to answer Becky's question. The girls were far too young to understand the importance of their father's job.

"Not for a long time. Maybe never, Beck," Rex replied.

"I don't want him to go back. Ever. And I don't want him to go to heaven and leave me here." Becky's sobs turned into gasps and hiccups.

Liza's lips began to quiver as her sister's distress agitated her. Juliana feared the children might never settle. Her gaze landed on the guitar in a corner. She'd noticed the guitar case in the back of the closet when she'd moved into Rex's home and then she'd spotted the instrument in the corner when she'd brought the girls home earlier tonight. What had made Rex drag it out? He'd claimed music was no longer part of his life. Had that changed?

"Why don't you sing to her?"

Rex's head jerked toward her. "What?"

"Sing for her. It might calm her down. I've been playing your CDs in the car and she likes your music."

In the dim illumination from the streetlights streaming through the front window, she could see his jaw muscles bunching and shifting. He swallowed hard and grimaced as if he were in pain. Finally, he exhaled. "You want that, Beck?"

Becky nodded.

"Me, too. Me, too," Liza added.

Rex sat Becky on the sofa and crossed the room with a stiff stride. Every muscle in his bare back above his hastily pulled on jeans looked knotted. Juliana wondered if she'd misread the significance of the guitar coming out of the closet. Moments later, he returned with the instrument, settled on the ottoman and hesitated.

Becky scooted against Juliana's side. Liza burrowed deeper into Juliana's lap. The sweet smell of the girls' strawberry-scented bubble bath encircled her and she felt a twinge of sadness. Her mother had missed moments like this. Soothing nighttime fears had been Irma's job.

"Do you need a lamp on?" Juliana asked as she tucked Becky beneath her arm.

"No." His voice sounded rough, raw. He strummed a few chords, stopped and started again. And then he sang, low and husky, gaining strength as the song progressed. The girls settled. Rex lifted his eyes and his gaze locked with Juliana's as he transitioned into a song she hadn't heard before, one about a man wanting to put the past behind him and live again.

There was something so inherently sexy about a bare-chested, barefoot man cradling a guitar in the near-darkness and singing about starting over that Juliana's insides melted.

Rex's up-tempo songs kept her toes tapping on her daily commute, but his ballads often brought tears to her eyes as this one did tonight. For a man who didn't talk much, Rex's magical way with words entranced her. What would it be like to be serenaded by the man she loved, to hear his deepest feelings expressed in lyrics and music? She'd never know.

Several songs later, Rex drew to a close and set the guitar aside. It was only then that the mesmerizing spell he'd cast over her broke and Juliana realized both girls had fallen back to sleep.

"Let's get them to bed." Rex rose. His hands brushed her hip and thigh, electrifying her, as he lifted Becky.

After they tucked the girls in and returned to their room, Juliana faced Rex in the moonlight. "That was beautiful. I don't know how you gave it up."

He shoved his hands in his pockets. "I walked away because I didn't like the person I'd become."

"I don't understand."

His hands fisted and his rigid body language warned Juliana she might not like whatever he said next. "On the night we met, you asked me if I had jealous husbands chasing me. I said not anymore. But I used to. After a show, I'd indiscriminately screw any woman that my manager brought into my dressing room. I don't remember their names or their faces. I used them and discarded them like paper cups. Like they were worthless."

Shocked into silence, Juliana could only stare at him. So the Internet stories had been true.

"I didn't care if they were married or single. All I cared about was letting off steam, coming down from my post-concert high. Other folks used drugs. I used sex. I used *people.*"

The man she'd come to know over the past three weeks bore no resemblance to the self-absorbed person he described. But there was more than sordid truth in Rex's confession. Juliana heard pain and self-loathing in his voice.

He shoved a hand through his tangled hair. "My behavior shamed and disgusted my family. Hell, I probably even broke up a few marriages."

His wounded gaze lasered in on hers. He expected his revelation to repulse her. "Now you know why you need to stay the hell away from me. I'm a selfish jerk who doesn't know how to have a healthy relationship with a woman. I'm not good enough for you, Juliana, and if you're half as smart as I think you are then you'll pack your stuff, get out and forget you ever met me."

And she knew in an instant that she couldn't do as he asked. She wasn't just in lust with Rex Tanner. She was falling in love with him.

Nine

Why didn't Juliana tell him to go to hell?

Why didn't she flee his apartment in disgust?

Wasn't that what he expected? What he wanted? Yeah, because the sooner she dumped him, the sooner he could quit waiting for it to happen.

But instead of revulsion in Juliana's beautiful blue eyes, Rex found understanding and a tangle of emotions he couldn't decipher on her moonlit face. She closed the distance between them and lifted her palms to blaze a path across his chest, and then she cradled his face in her hands, tugged him down and peppered soft kisses over his face and finally on his mouth.

His pulse drummed in the triple digits. The blood drained from his head to pool with an insistent throb behind his zipper.

He covered her hands and drew back. "What are you doing?"

Her soft, sexy gaze met his and a tender smile trembled on her lips. "Loving you."

His heart stalled and then slammed against his ribs like automatic gunfire. "Me? Or the guy with the guitar?"

Her thumbs rasped over his bristly jaw. "The guy who just sang his nieces to sleep. The one who gets inside me with his words and melts me with his touch. The man who taught me to take control of his Harley and my life. You, Rex Tanner."

He couldn't comprehend half of what she said, but couldn't string the words together to ask her to explain. A knot formed in his throat. He gulped it down. "Bad idea."

"I can't think of a better one." And then her tongue coasted across his bottom lip, igniting the fuse of desire in his veins.

Her fingers threaded through his hair and Rex struggled to recall the reasons why this shouldn't happen. Music was part of it. He didn't want to go back on the road, but as far as he could see, he only had two options. Tour or lose the bar.

In the first case, he'd hurt Juliana by reverting to his previous bad habits. He'd like to believe he wouldn't, but he had ten years of proof that he probably would. But even if he could control the selfish beast inside him, he'd still be on the road nine months out of the year. A beautiful woman like Juliana wouldn't sit at home alone waiting for him. He'd seen the marriages of his band and crew members disintegrate for exactly that reason. Lonely wives were unhappy wives.

In the latter case, he'd cause a rift between her and her family. Juliana's mother had barely tolerated him at the auction. She wouldn't accept a washed-up country star or a bar owner—especially a broke one who owed her bank money—as a son-in-law.

Son-in-law.

Whoa. He rocked back on his heels. His gaze hungrily devoured Juliana's damp lips and flushed cheeks.

Was he thinking marriage? With Juliana.

Hell, yes. But how could he make it work? He couldn't.

Juliana's teeth nipped his jaw and her palm stroked over the hard ridge beneath his jeans, making thought impossible. Later. He'd try to figure out how to make this relationship work *later.* Right now he needed her, ached for her, and it had nothing to do with pent-up excitement from playing music. This was all about her. Her scent. Her taste. Her acceptance of him, warts and all.

He banded his arms around her, holding her as tightly against himself as he could get her, and seized her mouth, pouring his feelings into the kiss, showing what he couldn't say. He raked his palms up and down her spine, savoring her shiver, and then he cupped her butt and buried his erection in the heat of her belly. Nothing had ever felt this good.

He bunched her robe in his fists, lifting an inch at a time until the fabric was out of the way and he could stroke smooth, bare bottom. Her gasp incited him. Still it wasn't enough. He wanted to hear her whimper and cry out as orgasm rocked her. The sounds she made when he pleasured her were almost enough to get him off.

Naked. He needed her naked. *Now.* He shucked her robe and palmed her breasts, teasing the tight, beaded tips. Her head fell back, exposing her throat to his lips. He sucked and nipped her fragrant skin and laved the fluttering pulse at the base of her neck. Still not enough. He eased his hand between them and found her curls, her moisture. He devoured her mouth, gulping down her moans as he stroked her until she squirmed and then quaked against him.

Her nails scraped over his back, making him shake all over, and then she fumbled with the opening of his jeans and shoved his pants and briefs down his thighs. Urgent and hurried, her soft fingers skated over his butt, his waist, his hips, and then she wrapped her hand around him and caressed him from base to tip, damn near blowing off the top of his head in an ecstatic shower of sparks. He yanked his head back to gasp and groan.

She dropped to her knees to help him out of his jeans and then her dangerous hands made the return trip, feathering his legs with a light touch until she reached the tops of his thighs. Juliana tipped her head back and met his gaze as she took him into her mouth.

Holy spit. He didn't deserve this. Didn't deserve *her.*

His hands fisted in her hair and every muscle in his body clenched as he fought to hold on, but the silken swirl of her tongue nearly undid him. Fire roared through him and he nearly let go, but more than his own satisfaction, he wanted to give Juliana pleasure. He yanked her to her feet, nudged her backward until she fell on the bed and then he hit his knees and loved her with his mouth—something he'd never done for the groupies. She tasted hot and wet and sweet and uniquely Juliana.

Her moans and pleas sounded like music to his ears as he played her into one release and then another. And then he rose above her, parted her legs and sank into her in one long, deep stroke.

Heaven.

No doubt about it, he could learn to love it here. Hell, he already did. He withdrew and sank back in. Again. Again. Her silky legs encircled his hips and her heels dug into his buttocks. She wiggled beneath until he thought he'd go insane. He swallowed her cries as he pounded out a rhythm guaranteed to drive them both over the edge. His lungs burned. His heart raced. His skin dampened, melding with hers.

Her wandering hands wreaked havoc on his self-control. She stroked, scraped, brushed and squeezed. And he knew he was going to lose it. *Hold on, hold on.* He bowed his back to sip one tight pearly nipple and then release rippled through Juliana. Rex said a prayer of thanks as her cry filled his ears and then he let go. A series of explosions began at the base of his spine and detonated upward.

He collapsed. Boneless. Totally wiped out.

Totally in love.

Oh hell.

"I'm in love with her." The words erupted from Rex's chest like a volcano that had built up so much pressure it had no choice but to blow.

Kelly blinked and then turned to her husband, who'd stretched out on a lawn chair in their backyard. The girls danced around him in the grass, raining kisses and questions. Other than being ten shades too pale, Rex thought his brother-in-law was a damned fine sight. His broken bones would mend and the bruises would fade. Whether or not he could return to active duty remained to be determined.

"Mike, Rex and I are going inside to get some cold drinks." She pointed at Rex. "You. Kitchen. Now."

Rex followed her inside, already regretting his outburst, but the words had been expanding inside him since last night. He hadn't said anything to Juliana because he'd needed to digest them and to plan first. The right thing to do would be to let her go. He wasn't a prize and she sure as hell deserved better. But how could he walk away?

Kelly handed him a beer. "Spill it."

Rex passed the bottle back. "It's 10:30. Too early for drinking."

"I want to loosen your tongue." But she put the beer back in the fridge. "Start talking or I'll pour the beer down your throat."

He swiped a hand over his hair. "I'm in love with Juliana Alden. She's a banking heiress, for crying out loud. Too good for a high-school dropout like me. And I'm thinking about going back on the road."

Wariness clouded Kelly's face. "Okay. One thing at a time. Do you want to tour again?"

"No."

"Then don't."

"I think I want to marry Juliana."

Kelly growled in frustration. "I'm trying to follow your train of thought here, Rex, but you're not making it easy. What's stopping you from marrying Juliana? The girls adore her, by the way."

He paced the confines of the tiny kitchen. "I need the money. The bar's not making it, Kel. It might in time, but I don't have time. The note's coming due."

She slapped his arm. "You have money, moron."

"If I did, we wouldn't be having this conversation. And if I ask Juliana to marry me when I'm about to default on a loan to her family's bank, then she and her folks will think I'm doing it because of the money."

"You have your part of Mom and Dad's estate."

He balked. "That's not mine. When I left the ranch I forfeited my share."

"Dang it, Rex, you sent money home every year for ten years—money Dad used to keep the ranch going. I tried to discuss this with you after the funeral, but you tuned me out and the lawyer says his letters came back unopened. In fact…" She held up one finger. "Wait here."

She left the room and returned a moment later to hand him a file. "Here's all the account info. See if it's enough to tide you over until Renegade's in the black."

He opened the file and surprise punched the air from his lungs. It wasn't a fortune, but it was more than enough to pay off his loan. But it wasn't his.

"I remember telling you to save this for you and the girls in case something happened to Mike." He didn't need to mention the close call they'd just had. "You keep it."

He tried to give her the file, but she put her hands behind

her back. "It's not mine. It's yours. Mike has life insurance. Don't let your pride screw up your future."

Pain crushed his chest. "Kelly, I don't deserve this. I was an ass."

"I know. I was there. But Mom and Dad loved you, Rex. They always loved you, and they understood your need for your songs to be heard. They were so proud of you. We all were. We weren't crazy about your lifestyle…." She shrugged. "But that was because we were afraid you'd kill yourself."

He grimaced. "You can't say I didn't try."

"Rex, you've never been afraid to fight for what you wanted. So why aren't you fighting now?"

Good question.

"Pride has always been your biggest problem, big brother. So…swallow your pride, take the money and go get the girl."

"She deserves better than me, Kel."

"That's what being in love is all about—trying to be the person the one you love deserves." She hooked her arms around his waist and hugged him. "And stop punishing yourself for the past by denying yourself the music you love. There's bound to be a way you can have music in your life without doing concerts."

She lifted a hand and tugged on his hair. "And quit hiding that handsome mug from the world under all this. Let me give you a real haircut. I've been dying to do more than trim your ends for ages."

Hiding. Yeah. That's what he'd been doing. And Juliana had dragged him out of his cave and back into the light.

The question was did he have the guts to lay his heart on the line?

If Emily Post covered guidelines on how to end an almost-engagement, then none of the etiquette lessons Juliana had endured during her formative years had included them.

As far as she was concerned, no matter what she served, lunch would be hard to swallow. She put the finishing touches on the lemon chicken and roasted asparagus she'd picked up from Wally's favorite restaurant and then brightened the chandelier in her dining room. Intimacy wasn't her goal for this private meeting.

She loved Rex Tanner. In that blinding moment of discovery last night, Juliana's past mistakes had become clear. She'd never taken a chance on love because she'd been afraid of letting emotion overrule logic, but playing it safe hadn't made her stronger or smarter than her friends and colleagues who'd nursed numerous broken hearts over the years. Playing it safe had made her an emotional coward.

She didn't fool herself into believing her decision wouldn't have repercussions—difficult ones. First and foremost, she'd disappoint her mother—never a pleasant experience, but Juliana wasn't a child who feared being shipped away to boarding school anymore. She might even lose her job at Alden's, but despite the fact that she'd never wanted to work anywhere else, she'd rather lose her job than lose Rex.

And, yes, saying goodbye to Wally could jeopardize the merger that Alden's needed to stay competitive with the conglomerate banks, because Mr. Wilson was the type to hold grudges. But this wasn't the Middle Ages. Businesses could merge without families doing the same.

Beginning today, she would make new plans for her future—a future she hoped to spend with Rex. He hadn't said he loved her, but no man could be as tender, as devoted to her pleasure or as concerned about hurting her as he was unless he had deep feelings for her. If he didn't care for her, then he would have used and discarded her as he had the groupies in his past. Instead, her reluctant rebel had tried to scare her off with words while his eyes had begged for understanding.

Tonight she'd tell him she loved him. And tomorrow... Her mouth dried and her pulse fluttered. Tomorrow she'd deal with the consequences of her decision.

The doorbell rang and Juliana's stomach plunged to her pumps. Her guest had arrived. Pulling a painful breath into her tight chest, she prayed for the courage to take a huge risk. With her future. With her heart.

She opened the door. "Hello, Wally. Thanks for agreeing to come over for lunch."

He revealed a practiced smile and pulled a bouquet of red roses from behind his back. "As always, I'm happy to accommodate you, Juliana."

Why hadn't she noticed how smooth he was before? Too smooth, too polished, too pleasant. His smile didn't even crinkle the corners of his eyes. Not that Wally wasn't handsome. He was in a catalogue-model kind of way— good-looking enough to catch a woman's eye, but not enough to threaten a man.

Safe. That's it. Wally was safe, she realized with a flash of insight. No wonder she'd agreed to consider marrying him.

She accepted the flowers. "Thank you. Please come in. I'll put these in water. Would you care for a drink before lunch?"

"No, thank you. I have a meeting later. You have to return to work as well, don't you?"

"Yes." Although she probably wouldn't be able to focus any better than she had this morning. "Have a seat in the dining room. I'll bring out lunch."

Five minutes later, she had the meal on the table, the flowers in a Waterford vase and a swarm of angry hornets ricocheting around her stomach. She doubted she'd be able to swallow a single bite.

Wally launched into a discussion about his latest work project—a project that would have fascinated Juliana a few weeks ago. Andrea was right. She and Wally never discussed anything but work. Her lack of participation must have finally dawned on him. "So, Juliana what's this impromptu lunch really about?"

Soften the rejection. But her mind emptied of anything except the unpleasant task ahead. She folded her napkin and laid it beside her plate. "Are you and Donna enjoying your Saturday suppers?"

"Yes, as a matter of fact, we are. And are you enjoying your riding lessons?"

She couldn't remember seeing that sparkle in Wally's eyes before. "Yes. Even more than the lessons, I've enjoyed baby-sitting for Rex's nieces. Spending time with the girls has made me eager to have children of my own. That's not something I've ever dwelled upon. It seemed like a vague possibility for the very distant future."

"Not so distant. You're already thirty. And I'm forty." His soft hand covered hers on the table and she felt nothing except a strong urge to move away. "We need to get started. We'll make beautiful children together, Juliana."

Anxiety closed her throat. Juliana withdrew her hand, sipped—gulped, actually—her water and took a bracing breath. "I appreciate the time you've spent with me and your patience while waiting for me to come to a decision about us, but I'm sorry, Wally. I can't marry you."

Panic flashed in his eyes and then his expression turned placid, albeit a little flushed. "Of course you can. We're perfectly suited."

His refusal to accept her rejection surprised her. "I don't love you."

"I don't love you, either, but I expect our feelings will change over time."

Why did his blunt confession take her aback? She'd

been thinking the same way until recently. "Wally, I love someone else."

His brows dipped. "Your bachelor?"

"Yes. Rex Tanner."

"Your mother is no more likely to accept him into the bosom of the family than mine is to welcome Donna."

Juliana gaped. "Donna? You love Donna?"

Wally lowered his gaze and fidgeted with his silverware. "I've been in love with Donna since the first day she set foot in my office, but I never acted on my feelings until the auction forced them into the open." A tender smile flickered on his lips—the kind Juliana had never seen directed at her. "I don't know whether to bless you or curse you for that. But the fact remains, the Donnas and Rexes of this world would never be accepted into our social circle."

"That's a risk I'm willing to take."

His chin set in a stubborn line and his eyes hardened. "Then you're being foolish. Look at what you stand to lose. My father would disown me if I married Donna. Your mother is likely to do the same if you marry your bar owner."

"I know." The weight of that knowledge sat heavily in her stomach. "Wally, I've spent my entire life trying not to disappoint my mother, but by playing it safe I also insulated myself from the real world. I've been watching from the sidelines instead of experiencing life firsthand. I don't want to do that anymore."

He leaned back in his seat. "Then we'll compromise. We'll marry. Our families and our businesses will benefit. I'll turn a blind eye to any *hobbies* you might have if you'll do the same. We will of course need to present a grandchild or two relatively soon to make our parents happy, but beyond that, you may live your life in any way you see fit as long as you're discreet."

Dumbfounded, Juliana could only stare at Wally. He couldn't possibly be suggesting what she thought he was. Could he?

He reached into his pocket and pulled out a small, square blue box. *A ring box.*

Someone knocked at the front door, but Juliana's muscles wouldn't obey the order to get up and answer it. *Was he out of his mind?* A proposal followed in the same breath as a statement of his intentions to commit adultery and permission granting her the same freedom. This was a side of Wally—a distasteful side—Juliana had never seen before.

Wally opened the box, revealing the largest, gaudiest diamond Juliana had ever seen about the same time a key grated in the lock and her front door swung open. Rex stepped inside. His gaze sought and quickly found hers, and then one dark sweeping glance took in the meal, the flowers and the ostentatious boulder in Wally's extended hand.

Rex's jaw tightened and his eyes turned hard and cold.

Horrified, Juliana bolted to her feet. "Rex, it's not what you think."

And then she saw what he'd done. "Your hair. You cut your hair."

The windblown, carefree style wasn't banker short by any means. The long layers covered his ears and brushed his collar, accentuating his square jaw. If anything, he looked even more handsome than before.

She took a step toward him but Wally rose, blocked her path and faced Rex. "I'm Wallace Wilson, Juliana's fiancé. And you are her bachelor, correct?"

Rex's gaze shifted from her to Wally and back again. Every muscle in his body looked knotted.

"You're not my fiancé, Wally," Juliana corrected.

"That's only because we were interrupted before I put my ring on your finger." He held the ring where Rex couldn't miss it. "We've been unofficially engaged for months. Your mother has already booked the church and the caterers and set the date. On October twenty-first you'll be my bride."

That sounded like her mother. When all else failed, bulldoze. But Wally? Wally had never been the bulldozer type.

"I don't want to marry you, Wally. I'm sorry, but I don't and I won't." She pushed her way around him and approached Rex. "I wasn't going to accept his proposal."

Rex's nostrils flared and his lips flattened into a straight line. "How long have you been dating him?"

"Six months, but—"

"And you've been seeing him—*engaged to him*—while you've been sleeping with me?"

Juliana always, *always* trusted facts, but she had to admit the facts did not look good at the moment. "Not exactly, we—"

"So what was I? A walk on the wild side like the reporter said?"

"Yes. *No!*" How could she explain? "Rex, it started out that way, but then I fell in love with you."

He'd wanted to hear those words. God, he'd wanted to hear them, but Rex couldn't believe them now.

He should have trusted his gut. What they had was too good to be true. He'd never been faithful to a woman before Juliana. Why had he expected fidelity? What in the hell made him think he deserved it?

Juliana had told him about the pressure of her family's expectations and her dissatisfaction with her "nice" life, but she'd deliberately kept quiet about the perfect fiancé waiting in the wings. She'd used Rex—*used him*—to scratch her restless itch.

The pain shredding his insides was indescribable. He never would have expected his—*not his, dammit*—rule-following banker to lie. He had to get out of here. He pitched Juliana's house key onto the hall table, pivoted on his heel and headed out the door.

"Rex, wait." Juliana followed him outside and down the sidewalk. She planted herself between him and his truck in the driveway. "Please, let me explain."

"If he's your fiancé, then you've said enough."

"He's not. Not officially."

Not officially. What in the hell did that mean? Forget it. He didn't want to know.

"My parents want me to marry Wally to cement a merger between his family's bank and Alden's. I agreed to see if Wally and I suited. That's all. I never agreed to marry him. And I invited him here today to tell him that I couldn't marry him. I had no idea he'd bring a ring."

Yeah, right. A man didn't spend that kind of money without some encouragement. The damned ring probably cost more than Rex had borrowed from the bank to start up Renegade.

"Juliana, you run from your parents rather than speak your mind. Were you hoping he'd refuse to take my cast-offs and save you having to find the guts to tell your mother no?"

He hardened himself to the pallor of her face and the quiver of her painted lips.

"No. No, it was never that. But you're right. I never had the courage to defy my parents before. Not until I bought your auction package. I'm not good at defiance and I hate confrontation unless I have the facts to back up my arguments. But I don't love Wally and I won't marry him, no matter how much my mother wishes otherwise. I love *you,* Rex, and I will do anything—*anything*—to be with you."

She was one hell of an actress. The pain in her eyes and the sincerity in her voice looked and sounded real.

"You used me for a cheap thrill. You're no better than a

groupie." No better than he'd been when he'd used and discarded women. His chest tightened until he could barely draw a breath, and he hurt all over as if he'd been run over by a tour bus. If this is how the women he'd used felt, then he ought to be shot. Another wave of self-disgust washed over him.

"Rex, I love you. You have to believe me." She lifted a hand to cup his jaw. He intercepted it, lowered it back to her side and released her. He would not allow her touch to confuse the issue because when she touched him, he couldn't think straight.

He'd been a fool to think a rich, educated *heiress* could be happy with a guy like him. Juliana belonged with the kind of guy who could buy her a skating rink of a ring. A guy who wouldn't drive a wedge between her and her family.

That guy wasn't him.

"That's the problem, Juliana. I can't believe anything you say anymore."

He clasped her upper arms, moved her aside and climbed in his truck. He shot one last glance at her as he put the vehicle in motion and wished he hadn't.

Damn, those tears looked real.

Life on the road and out of Wilmington looked better every minute.

Ten

"Why did you call this meeting, Juliana?" Margaret Alden glanced at the mantel clock of the Alden living room as if she had somewhere she'd rather be. It had always been that way.

Irma had filled in for Margaret at Juliana's school functions, and the nanny had been the one who'd played dolls with Juliana, taught her to cook, how to apply makeup and do her hair. Irma had been the mother Juliana's mother had been too busy to be. Juliana didn't want to be that kind of mother to her own children—if she ever had any. Her pulse stuttered and her mouth dried. Her chance might come sooner than expected.

She swallowed, but her nausea refused to subside, and then she glanced at her father and brother. She wanted to go home, climb under the covers and cry her eyes out over the disastrous encounter with Rex. But that would only lead to another headache.

Her lack of courage was what had led her here. It was time

to stand up for herself. She took a deep breath. "I'm not marrying Wally. I had lunch with him Monday and told him the engagement is off."

Her mother set her wineglass down so abruptly it was a wonder the base didn't snap. "Are you out of your mind? Do you realize what this could do to the Alden-Wilson merger?"

Be strong. Mother goes for the jugular at any sign of weakness. "The banks can merge without a marriage. I am not a stock option or an asset to be traded in the deal. I'm your daughter. And I'm in love with someone else."

"The biker?" High-pitched horror raised her mother's voice.

"Rex Tanner, the bachelor I bought at your auction."

"He's totally unsuitable."

"For you maybe, but not for me."

"Eric, talk some sense into your sister."

"I can't do that, Mother. If Juliana's in love, then she needs to follow her heart. You tried to barter me in the deal and I was stupid enough to go along with it. The best thing that ever happened to me was having Priscilla run off."

Juliana turned toward Eric so quickly she nearly gave herself whiplash. What had changed his mind? No, she didn't want to know. Not if Holly was involved. Her brother went through women like most men went through neckties. She couldn't handle her best friend becoming one of his cast-offs.

Yes, she could. And she'd be there to pick up the pieces and help Holly through it. That's what friends were for.

"Richard," her mother screeched at Juliana's father.

"I agree with Eric. Juliana needs to follow her heart. The bank is strong enough to survive with or without the merger if Wilson turns pigheaded. When do I get to meet this Reg, Juliana?"

Another surprise. Juliana could count on one hand the times her father had gone against her mother's wishes and still have the majority of her fingers left over. Juliana wanted to kiss him.

"His name is Rex. And you won't get to meet him unless I can make him understand this convoluted situation. He found out about Wally and he's angry. Right now he won't accept my phone calls. But I love him, so I'm not giving up yet."

She'd phoned and left messages for two days, but Rex hadn't returned her calls. Today his message machine hadn't picked up, so she'd driven to Renegade during her lunch hour to talk to him, but it was his day off and Danny, the bartender, had said Rex was out.

She had to find him and make him understand. Especially now. Her period was late. Juliana couldn't remember one single time in her life when her body hadn't run like a well-organized calendar.

Was she pregnant? Her pulse jigged erratically and panic threatened to choke her. They'd used protection every single time except the night Becky's cries had woken them. She'd known since junior-high health class that once was enough.

Did she want to be pregnant? She touched a hand to her agitated stomach and took in a slow, calming breath. Thoughts of having Rex's baby excited and worried her. She wanted a man who loved her, not a man who married her because of a misplaced sense of duty. She wouldn't force Rex to be with her for the sake of a baby.

Then there would be the fallout from this conversation to deal with. Her mother's pinched expression didn't bode well. If her mother couldn't forgive her, then Juliana might find herself alone, pregnant and out of a job. Certainly, she had her savings account, the remainder of her trust fund and investments to fall back on, but those wouldn't last indefinitely. She'd have to get another job, and she wanted more for her child than a single parent who worked sixty-hour weeks. Rex had shown her what she'd missed as a child and no baby of hers would take second place to a career.

Her mother's sharp gaze landed on Juliana's hand. Juliana faked smoothing a wrinkle from her linen skirt. No need to raise a panic before she knew for sure. The first pregnancy-test result had been negative, but the instructions warned of the possibility of a false negative if the test were run too soon and suggested waiting a few days to run a second test. She had a second kit waiting in her bathroom at home. She'd never been an impatient person, but waiting until the weekend was excruciating.

She licked her dry lips. "That's all I had to say, but I wanted you to have the facts before going into the meeting with the Wilsons tomorrow. I hope you understand."

Her mother looked as inflexible as ever. "Juliana, you have never been the type to make illogical and impulsive decisions. For the good of the bank, you *will* rethink this matter."

"Mother, Wally's in love with someone else, too. I'm not going to ruin four lives for the sake of the bank. If you can't accept that then—" she swallowed the panic clawing her throat "—then I'll have to tender my resignation."

She didn't wait to hear the response to her ultimatum and probably couldn't have heard it anyway over her thundering pulse. Juliana picked up her purse and left.

"Visitor for you," Danny said from the office door Thursday evening.

Danny had told him about Juliana's earlier visit. "It's my day off. I'm not here."

"It's not Juliana."

And it wouldn't be John Lee. Rex had formally turned down his former manager's offer and driven him to the airport. Kelly and the girls needed Rex now more than ever while Mike was on the mend. Rex couldn't go back on the road and he couldn't spend the rest of his life running and hiding. Eventually, he'd have to come out of his office.

Danny waited by the door. "All right. I'm coming."

He rose and followed Danny out front. An attractive blonde waited at the end of the bar. He didn't know her. At least he didn't think he did. What if the women from his past saw Octavia's articles the way John Lee had and looked him up? He'd be apologizing for the rest of his life.

"Can I help you?"

"Rex?"

"Yeah. Do I know you?"

"No, we've never met."

Good, not a woman from his past. The knot between his shoulder blades eased.

"Excuse me a sec." She opened her cell phone and pushed a button, but didn't speak into the phone. "But I did see you at the bachelor auction. Nice haircut."

The front door opened. He glanced up and Juliana, looking like a slice of summer sky in a blue dress the color of her eyes, walked in. His stomach dropped and his pulse rate tripled. Adrenaline flooded his veins, but he tamped down the feeling. He was *not* happy to see her. She'd lied to him and betrayed him.

"Nice meeting you, Rex, and I hope to see more of you in the future, but I'm out of here." The blonde slid off the bar stool and then headed for the exit. "He's all yours. Call me," she said as she passed Juliana.

He could add being devious to Juliana's sins. She approached cautiously. With her pale skin and the dark bruise-like circles beneath her eyes, she looked as bad as he felt. He hardened his heart. Her conscience probably wouldn't let her sleep at night. "What do you want?"

"We need to talk."

"Nothing left to say."

"Rex." She looked over her shoulders and then met his gaze again. Agony and worry filled her eyes. "I'm late."

It took five seconds for her meaning to kick in. His legs threatened to give out. "Follow me."

He led her to the office with his mind and stomach competing in a back-flip competition. "Sit."

Her flowers-and-spice scent filled his lungs as she passed and his blood pooled behind his zipper. Dammit. How could she still get to him when he knew she'd lied to him?

He shut the door. "How late?"

"Just a few days."

"Have you done a test?"

"Yes. It's negative. But Rex, I've never been late. Ever. I'll run another test this weekend, but I thought…I thought you should know."

"So if slumming didn't get you out of the marriage you didn't want, you figured getting knocked up with my kid would?"

She stiffened. "I didn't get pregnant on purpose."

"Don't jump the gun. You might not be pregnant." He folded his arms across his chest. "Why didn't you have the balls to just say no to the marriage?"

Juliana dipped her head and knotted her fingers in her lap. "All my life I…I felt like my parents only loved me when I was perfect. The straight-A student, the ribbon-winning horseback rider, the most graceful debutante. Whenever I stepped out of line, my mother threatened to send me to school out of state. And I knew she'd do it. By the time I turned sixteen, several of my schoolmates had been exiled to boarding school."

The pencil snapped in his fingers. He pitched it in the trash. Did she expect him to buy that poor-little-rich-girl crap? "That has nothing to do with me."

"It does. When I bought you at the auction, I was rebelling. Yes, I know, thirty is a little late to get started, but it took me being backed into a corner to find my nerve. My mother cooked up her scheme for me to marry Wally to cement the Alden-Wilson merger. I felt like a commodity instead of a daughter. Worse, all the facts, all the logic pointed to the marriage being the sensible choice. I've always trusted facts more than emotions and the facts said to say yes."

Her eyes begged for understanding. "But I didn't want to. For once in my life, I wanted to experience the passion other women whisper about, even though I seriously doubted that I could since I've never…" Her cheeks flushed. "I figured that if I couldn't find what I was looking for with a man as blatantly sexy as you, then I was a lost cause, and I may as well marry Wally because I had nothing to lose."

He bit his tongue. The dragon lady couldn't be as bad as Juliana painted her, and if Juliana expected him to believe she'd never had good sex before him, then she probably expected him to believe in the tooth fairy.

"You bought me because you wanted to get laid? What made you think I'd be so easy?"

Pink tinged her pale cheeks. "You were right when you accused me of researching your past. From everything I'd read, you sounded like a guy who would get the job done and move on without thinking twice."

Damn. Didn't that just make his day?

"But then you weren't the rebel I'd read about. You weren't interested in corrupting me and you were a softie with Becky and Liza. But strangely, that made me want to be corrupted more than ever. I was physically attracted to you in a way that I'd never been to any other man, Rex. And I liked you."

Liked him. Why didn't she just stick a pin in his ego and deflate it?

"I have never chased a man in my life, and I chased you. I bought clothing that would give my father a heart attack, and I acted like…like a hussy."

Juliana wouldn't recognize a hussy if she passed one standing under a red light on the street corner. "That doesn't excuse what you did."

"No, it doesn't. I bought you with the intention of using you and walking away at the end of the month. And that's unforgivable. But if anyone can understand how much I regret that, then you should."

Whoa. Low blow. The woman fought dirty.

"Rex, my life was boring and empty until I met you. I don't want to give up what we have. And even though the facts say a boring, rule-following bean counter is not the right woman for you, my heart tells me I can be and that I will be if you'll give me a chance. I love you, Rex."

His molars clamped together. Why did his heart blip every time she said that? He still couldn't believe her. A woman who had everything couldn't fall for a guy like him. And then there was the poor-little-rich girl, *Mommy Dearest* mother and no-passion thing. Juliana was laying it on too thick even for a country bumpkin like him to believe.

"That doesn't change the facts. I'll do my part for this kid—if there is one. But that's it."

"But—"

"No buts. We're through. And if you're pregnant then I'll want a paternity test as soon as possible. I won't pay child support for Wilson's kid."

She flinched and pressed a hand to her chest. "I've never slept with Wally."

"Tell it to someone who cares."

The problem was that someone was him. But he'd get over it. "You know your way out."

As soon as the office door closed behind her, he spun in his office chair and picked up his guitar.

"What is this?"

Juliana picked up her briefcase and looked at her mother. Her heart skipped a few beats then raced. "A pregnancy test."

"I can see that. Why do you have it?"

Her mother hadn't fired her for dumping Wally, but this might be the final straw. "Mom, you came over to give me a ride to work while my car's in the shop, not to paw through my trash or put me through an inquisition."

"I did not paw through your trash. This was in the bathroom wastebasket. On top. Are you expecting that man's baby?"

That man, said in that contemptuous tone, rubbed Juliana the wrong way. "Rex. His name is Rex. And I don't know yet."

"And what will you do if you are?"

Was it too early in the day to develop a stress headache? And did she dare take anything for it if she was pregnant? She needed to buy a pregnancy book. Just in case. "I don't know. Rex and I will work out something."

If he'd ever speak to her again.

"I know a discreet doctor—"

"I'm not having an abortion!"

"You'd rather disgrace your family by having a child out of wedlock?"

"Single women have children all the time these days, Mother. It's no big deal anymore." But it was to Juliana. If there was a baby, then she wanted her child to have two loving parents.

"I will not have a bastard grandchild."

The words were a true wake-up call. Her own passivity had led her mother to believe she had the right to make Juliana's decisions. "Mother, *you* will not have a choice. This is my decision and only my decision."

"One you will live to regret." Her mother marched out of the town house. Juliana followed. The ride to work passed in icy silence. She hated the tension between them, but none of this would have happened if her mother had ever opened the lines of communication or if Juliana had dared to assert her independence a decade ago.

She climbed from the car and stopped her mother outside the bank by touching her hand. "Mother, believe it or not, I didn't go into that auction with the intention of hurting you. And I would like to have your support in whatever choices I make about my future."

The pinched look around Margaret's mouth wasn't new, but the concern in her eyes was. Her fingers briefly squeezed Juliana's. "You have no idea what you're getting yourself into, and you're fooling yourself if you think illegitimacy won't have negative repercussions for you or the child."

Two hours later, Juliana sat at her desk with her third cup of decaf coffee at her elbow. It just didn't pack the same eye-opening punch as caffeinated brew. She'd finally managed to make sense of the spreadsheet in front of her when Eric strode in looking furious.

"Tell me she's wrong."

"Who and wrong about what?"

"Mother says that bastard knocked you up."

Beyond Eric, she could see her administrative assistant's eyes widen. "Could you close the door, please?"

He did and then he turned back to her desk with fury in every stiff line of his body. What was up with Eric? Her brother was usually cool and calm no matter what the circumstances.

"I don't know if I'm pregnant yet."

"Is he going to marry you?"

"He says he's not."

"Son of a bitch. I'll kill him."

"Eric, there are extenuating circumstances you don't understa—"

But her brother turned and stormed out without waiting for Juliana's explanation. The hornets in her belly took flight. This was *so* not good. She yanked open her desk drawer, grabbed her purse and raced out of her office. No time for the elevator. She ran down two flights of stairs and made it to the lobby before remembering she didn't have a car. Flustered and in a panic, Juliana sprinted back upstairs to her office.

"Heather, can I borrow your car?" she huffed to her assistant.

Since this wasn't a request Juliana had ever made before, Heather looked suitably confused.

"My brother is going to kill my—" Her what? What was Rex exactly? "—my lover if I don't stop him," Juliana explained. That sounded melodramatic, but she was too frazzled to search for saner words at the moment.

Heather dug out her keys and tossed them across the desk. "Good luck. Blue Honda. Third row."

Juliana blessed the traffic gods for their favors as she sped through town, catching all green lights and driving well over the speed limit for the first time in her life. Eric's SUV was the only car parked in front of Renegade—not surprising since the bar hadn't opened for the lunch crowd yet. Juliana parked, leaped from Heather's car and ran inside. The place was empty. She heard a thud and a grunt coming from the direction of Rex's office and darted in that direction.

She skidded to a stop at the end of the hall in time to see Rex block Eric's right fist. Eric quickly swung his left and again Rex intercepted.

"Stop it!" she screamed.

Her cry distracted Rex for a split second. His gaze met hers. Eric landed a blow, snapping Rex's head back. Rex staggered a few steps and then righted himself. Blood oozed from his split bottom lip.

"Eric, *stop.*" Eric ignored her and took another swing, which Rex deflected. Juliana sprang forward, putting herself between her brother and Rex. "I said stop."

As badly as she wanted to check on Rex and assess his

injuries, she didn't dare look away from Eric in case he tried to hit Rex again. Had her brother gone crazy?

"I will break you, you sorry son—"

"Then you'll break me, too, Eric. I love him. And I won't stand by while you or Mother or anyone else tries to harm Rex for something that's my fault. Yes, *my* fault," she added when Eric's eyes narrowed. "Get the whole story before you go off half-cocked again."

Eric's fists unclenched. The men acted like two wolves ready to fight over territory. Juliana risked a glance at Rex. His bottom lip was already swelling. She dug in her purse for a tissue and pressed it to the trickle of blood. He jerked his head out of her reach but accepted the tissue.

He didn't even trust her to touch him. That hurt. "I'm sorry. This is my fault. It's entirely my fault."

Eric snorted. "How in the hell do you figure that? This bastard used you."

"No Eric, I used him. I bought Rex and I seduced him."

Her brother choked a sound of disbelief. "Like I'd believe that."

His incredulity insulted her. "Well you should. It's the truth. And you owe Rex an apology."

"Like hell. If he's innocent, then why didn't he fight back?"

Rex pitched the bloody tissue into the trash. "Because my daddy always said if you do the crime, then you'd better be man enough to take your punishment. I slept with your sister and if she's pregnant, I may be the father of her child. And no, I won't marry her. I deserve your anger. Bring it on."

She spun to face him. "Are you insane?"

"Not anymore."

His acerbic tone implied he had been insane to be with her. The verbal jab slipped between her ribs with lethal stealth.

"I'm sorry, Rex. I am truly sorry that I hurt you. That was never my intention. Go back to work, Eric," she said without turning.

"Not without you."

She sighed. "Go. I'm right behind you."

After a pause, Eric's footsteps departed. Silence descended on the small office like a dense cloud of suffocating smoke.

"I'm sorry. I don't know what's wrong with Eric today. He's usually very even-tempered. I'll call you as soon as I know…as soon as I know whether or not I'm pregnant."

"I won't come between you and your family, Juliana. No matter what. I'll close Renegade and go back on the road first."

"Back on tour?"

"My former manager made me an offer this week."

Loss welled inside her. If he left, she'd never have a chance to change his mind. "You have to do what makes you happy, Rex. And if selling is what it takes…then I have contacts through the bank. I'll try to help you find a buyer."

Tears pricked the back of her eyes and a sob blocked her throat. She swallowed to subdue it, but it refused to disappear.

"But you're the one who told me that running never solves anything. If you can find it in your heart to forgive me, to give me a chance to prove my love, then I'll follow you anywhere. I'll quit my job—if I still have one—and live on a tour bus or wherever else you want. I don't care what my family thinks. I want you—" Her voice broke. She closed her eyes, struggled for composure and then met his gaze again. "I want you to be happy," she repeated, "even if it's not with me."

And then she left as quickly and quietly and with as much dignity as possible considering her world had just collapsed.

Nobody could act that well. Even an Oscar winner couldn't fake the pain Rex had seen in Juliana's eyes and heard in her voice.

She wanted him to be happy when she clearly wasn't.

She'd leave her family for him when pleasing them had ruled her life.

Doubt crushed him like a concert light bar falling from the stage scaffolding. Had Juliana been telling the truth? About her childhood, her mother, all of it? And if she was, then what next?

He flexed his fingers and the tight skin on his right hand pulled, making him wince. The pain came not from the punches he'd blocked, but from the blisters on his fingertips. Music had poured out of him since he'd caught Juliana with the *GQ* jerk. He'd barely been able to eat or sleep for the words and melodies playing in his head.

Writing songs had been his favorite part of the business, and if the past four days were anything to go by, then he hadn't lost the songwriting gift that had sold so many records. Hell, the stuff he'd written since losing Juliana was ten times better than anything he'd previously penned because his guts were all over the sheet music.

Maybe Kelly was right. Maybe he could have his music without touring.

Could he also have Juliana?

She claimed she loved him. Did she?

His heart kicked into a faster tempo.

Could a sophisticated debutante be happy with a high-school dropout? What did he have to offer a woman who had everything?

"You have a visitor," Danny said from the office door on Saturday afternoon.

Not again. The game was one Rex didn't want to replay. "I'm not here."

"It's not Juliana."

"Yeah. That's what you said last time."

"It's an older lady. She looks mean enough to flatten nails into sheet metal with her teeth. C'mon, man, she's scaring the customers."

Rex rose from behind the desk and followed Danny out front. The lunch crowd had ebbed, and the dinner crowd had yet to arrive. The third newspaper article had come out today. Because he and Juliana had canceled their appointment last Monday with Octavia, she'd left them out of her story this week, focusing instead on some of the other couples. If he had any luck at all, he wouldn't be harassed about riding a black motorcycle instead of a white horse today.

He heard his manager's voice say, "He'll be right out," about the same time he recognized his visitor. The dragon lady. Juliana's mother. Hell. He'd rather hear about the damned white horse.

Her eagle eyes—the same blue as Juliana's, but without the softness—beaded on him and her haughty posture turned rigid. Regal. He'd yet to figure out how these society women managed to look down their noses at somebody a foot taller than they were.

"Mrs. Alden."

"Mr. Tanner. Might I speak with you privately." It wasn't a question. It was a demand.

"My office is this way." He led her the short distance. "Have a seat."

The costly leather chairs, expensive desk and bookcases were relics from his Nashville days, and he had a feeling Mrs. Alden appraised each item within seconds of crossing the threshold.

She lowered herself into the visitor's seat. "I'll pay off your note if you'll stop seeing my daughter."

She didn't beat around the bush. Rex sat down and rocked back in his chair. "I've already stopped seeing Juliana, and I pay my own debts."

"I've taken the liberty of checking into your accounts. I don't see the reserves you'll need to make the payment on time."

"That's because my 'reserves' are not in your bank. In fact, I'll be closing all of my accounts with Alden's, beginning with the loan." He opened his desk drawer and withdrew the cashier's check he'd drawn this morning for the amount due on his note. Thanks to his inheritance, he could pay off his debts. He'd also set up college funds for Becky and Liza. He slid the check across the desk. "You've saved me a trip."

She didn't pick up the check. "I'll cancel your debt if you promise me you won't contact Juliana again."

"And what if she's carrying my kid?"

"That need not concern you. We'll handle it."

He sucked a sharp breath. How would they *handle* it if Juliana carried his baby? Would the dragon lady pressure Juliana into a decision they'd both regret? Anger, never far from the surface these past few days, boiled over. The fact that Mrs. Alden was every bit as overbearing as Juliana had described doubled his ire. Juliana hadn't lied about her mother. Did that mean she hadn't lied about anything else?

"Mrs. Alden, you can take your money and shov—"

"*Mr. Tanner,* don't say something you might regret. I will only make this offer once."

He rose and leaned over the desk, bracing himself on his fists. "Lady, you tried to sell your daughter, and now you're trying to buy me off. My opinion of you couldn't get any lower. If you have half a brain in your head, then you'd better start thinking about your daughter instead of your damned bank."

"I beg your pardon." He'd never seen a spine that stiff.

"It's not my pardon you need to be begging. It's Juliana's. Your actions are pushing her away and you're going to lose her if you don't wise up. The woman who bought me is one who's been stuck under your thumb for thirty years. It was only a matter of time before she got tired of your dictatorship and rebelled."

"I want what's best for Juliana."

"And you're damned sure I'm not it." He circled the desk and stretched to his full height, towering over the dragon lady. "What could be better for her than a man who worships her and would lay his heart at her feet? Because that's what you and your scheme have cost her."

Mrs. Alden rose stiffly, but Rex took satisfaction in taking a little starch out of her spine.

"You haven't heard the last from me, Mr. Tanner."

"No, ma'am, I probably haven't, but I have a news flash for you. If Juliana's carrying my baby, then you're not going to crush my child under your thumb like you did your daughter. I'll see you in hell first. And *that* is a promise you can take to the bank."

He snatched up the check and forced it into her hand, and then yanked open his office door.

Eleven

Another unpalatable meal.

Juliana wished she were anywhere except the exclusive waterfront restaurant with her mother. She'd awoken cranky and achy this morning, and to top it off she'd run the second pregnancy test with another negative result. She didn't know whether to be disappointed or relieved or to buy a third test on the way home. She wanted to know before she got her hopes up more than she had already.

She and her mother had never had the Sunday-brunch-meeting type of relationship—unless they were meeting for business. If her mother was going to fire her, then Juliana wished she'd get it over with. After almost an hour of meaningless chitchat Juliana just wanted to go home and crawl into her Whirlpool tub.

"Mother, why are we here?"

Her mother seemed more uncomfortable, more uncertain than Juliana had ever seen her before. "I realize I've not always been there for you, and I don't always understand your determination to do things the hard way, but I don't want to lose you, Juliana. Mr. Tanner seems to think I might."

Juliana blinked. "Excuse me? What does Rex have to do with this?"

"You're so like me. You're completely absorbed with your career and—"

"But I'm not you and I don't want to be you. I always thought I did, but recently, I realized how much you missed out on life." Juliana pressed her lips together and wished the words back. "I'm sorry. That was rude."

"And deserved, I'm afraid. I did miss much of yours and Eric's childhoods."

"We had Irma. But it would have been nice to have you, too."

"Yes, maybe, but I had so much to prove. Back in those days a woman had to work twice as hard as a man to make it to the top in the corporate world."

"Things have changed."

"In some ways, but you're still as naive about men as I was, Juliana."

"I don't understand."

"I was also a wealthy young woman. I had men vying for my attention. It quite turned my head. I fell in love. Twice. And each time, I eventually realized I wasn't the main attraction and my heart was broken. The men were after my daddy's money." She folded her napkin and laid it beside her plate, then lifted her gaze to Juliana's. "I didn't want that to happen to you."

Her mother had never discussed her past relationships. It seemed odd to hear these confidences now. "Maybe you should give me credit for being able to recognize the guys looking for an easy ride. I've dated and dumped my share. But that doesn't explain why you're so determined to push me into marriage with Wally."

"I wanted you to have a stable marriage based on compatibility in jobs and backgrounds. My father arranged a suitable marriage for me. I was trying to do the same for you and your brother to protect you from the pain I'd experienced."

Surprise stole her breath. "You didn't love Daddy when you married him? Not even a little?"

"I respected him and we had many common interests."

It sounded familiar and so sad. The relationship her mother described was exactly the kind of match Juliana and Wally had contemplated, and if Juliana hadn't met Rex, she'd probably be picking out china and silver patterns and settling for a life without love. Close call. Too close.

"If you don't love him, then why have you stayed with him for thirty-eight years?"

"Because I grew to love him. Not as ardently as you appear to love Mr. Tanner, but comfortably. We're like a matched pair of shoes. We function best together."

"Shoes?" How depressing. "As much as I like shoes, Mother, I don't want to live like one. I want more than that."

"Juliana, you could get hurt."

"I already hurt. I can't imagine the pain getting any worse. But you know what? I'd do it all again." Even knowing the outcome would be a broken heart, Juliana realized, she would risk loving Rex again. Gambling with a guaranteed bad result. A first for her. But then Rex had given her so many firsts.

"When did you talk to Rex?" If her mother had talked to him recently, then maybe he hadn't left town.

Juliana had never seen her mother squirm before today. Her cheeks darkened. "Yesterday. I tried to buy him off."

"You what?" Juliana squeaked in horror.

"My father tried to buy off each of the men who broke my heart and they took the money. That's how I knew they didn't love me. Your Mr. Tanner told me exactly where I could put my offer to cancel his business loan. Quite inappropriate, really."

Conflicting emotions battled inside her. Her mother had tried to get rid of Rex. And he'd refused. She pressed fingers to the smile trembling on her lips. Simultaneously, her eyes stung. "You shouldn't have done that."

"I've gone about this awkwardly, but I want what's best for you, my dear, and I thought I knew what that was. However, I was wrong. I suspect the right man for you might be Mr. Tanner. *Rex.*"

"It may be too late."

Her mother reached across the table and covered Juliana's hand. "It's never too late. And you are my daughter. If you're sure he's the man you want, then you'll find a way to win him."

"It's not that easy."

"Nothing worth having ever is. And if there is a baby, then we'll adjust. With or without a marriage. Shall we go? I imagine you need to contact Mr.—Rex."

"Mother, Rex hasn't even said he loves me."

"Then I imagine getting him to do so is your top priority."

The entire conversation seemed surreal. Juliana robotically followed her mother out to the car. Tomorrow was Monday, Rex's day off. Did she dare try one more time? Could she make him understand when the facts were stacked against her?

There were times when Juliana wished politeness hadn't been instilled into her from birth. This was one of those times. She wanted to ignore the doorbell and stay curled up on the sofa with her Swiss-chocolate-almond-flavored coffee.

Comfort coffee.

She wasn't pregnant.

She'd called in sick to work because she didn't know what to make of the aching disappointment when she'd made her discovery after lunch with her mother. She needed to discuss her confusing feelings with Andrea and Holly, and she'd called each of them earlier, but neither was at home. Just as well. What could she say? How could she explain her conflicting emotions?

The bell rang again, followed by a hard pounding on the wood. Reluctantly, she set down her mug, rose and shuffled on bare feet to the door. It was probably Eric or her father checking to see if she was all right. She looked through the peephole and her breath caught.

Rex.

Her heart thumped harder and her palms dampened. She smoothed them over her shorts. What did he want?

You'll never know if you don't open the door.

She glanced in the mirror over the hall table and winced. Her hair was tangled and her skin pale. She hadn't bothered with makeup. Even her nail polish was chipped because she'd been nibbling her nails. *You're a wreck.*

No time for repairs now.

She fumbled the lock and then turned the knob and opened the door. Air whooshed out of her lungs. Rex looked wonderful, tall and tanned with his jaw gleaming from a fresh morning shave. His lip was still a little swollen from Eric's punch. He wore his usual jeans and black boots, but today he'd pulled on a white western-style dress shirt with black onyx snaps—the kind he'd worn on his CD covers.

She couldn't read the expression in his dark eyes as they swept slowly over her face, breasts, belly and legs, and then back up again. Her skin tingled in the wake of his visual caress and she gulped.

"Good morning, Rex." So formal, when what she wanted to do was thread her fingers through his shorn hair and kiss him until they were both dizzy from lack of oxygen.

"'Morning." He shifted on his booted feet. "Can I come in?"

"Certainly." She stepped away from the door. His cologne teased her nose as he passed. She glanced out at her driveway because she hadn't heard the growl of his Harley and saw his pickup truck parked beside her sedan. Two motorcycles stood side by side in the truck bed.

Her pulse accelerated. Two bikes? What did that mean?

She closed the door and followed him into the den. The width of the room separated them. The distance seemed as vast as an ocean. *No use stalling. Say what you must. And then if he leaves… You'll deal with it.* "You didn't have to come over. I would have called later today. I'm not pregnant."

He inhaled sharply. "I'm sorry."

Confused, Juliana frowned. "Sorry I'm not pregnant?"

"Yeah. No." He swiped a hand through his hair, ruffling the strands the way she longed to. "Yeah."

He shook his head, looking as perplexed by his answer as she was. "I'd love to see you pregnant with my baby."

And that made absolutely no sense since he'd dumped her. Her heart fluttered as fast as a hummingbird's wings. The fact that he hadn't jumped for joy when she'd shared the news had to be a good sign, didn't it?

"How do you feel about it? About not being pregnant?" he asked with narrowed eyes.

Should she lie? No. She hugged her arms over her chest. "Disappointed."

"Why?"

"What do you mean, why?"

He closed the distance between them, stopping only inches away. The temptation to burrow into his broad chest and to wind her arms around his middle pulled at her.

"Do you want to have a baby? *My* baby?"

He shouldn't tease her like this. "Does it matter?"

"It does to me." His voice was low and quiet, barely a rumble of sound.

She scrubbed her upper arms, glanced away and then back again. "Yes. Yes, I'd like to have your baby."

His lips twitched and some of the stiffness left his shoulders as he exhaled. She hadn't even noticed his tension until she saw it drain away.

"Let's take a ride." He nodded toward her front door.

"Why?"

"I want to show you something. And I thought you might want to try soloing on the motorcycle. I have a bike for you in the back of the truck."

She wanted to go. Did that make her a glutton for punishment? Or could she take this opportunity to explain one more time that she loved him and had never intended to hurt him? She lifted her chin. She would not give up without a fight. "I need to change clothes."

"I'll wait."

Ten minutes later, she sat beside him in his truck wearing her low-rider jeans—because they were the only jeans she owned—and an untucked poplin shirt. The shirttails covered her belly. She hadn't dressed to seduce him. He needed to understand that he wasn't getting the sexy siren she'd pretended to be.

Miles passed before he spoke. "Your mother came to see me."

Juliana grimaced. "I know. I'm sorry. She didn't mean to insult you. She actually thought she was doing the right thing."

"Yeah." He sounded more amused than angry.

"And you won her over when you refused the money. Rex, I can't apologize enough. You've seen the absolute worst of my family this week. They—"

"Love you," he interrupted.

She considered the strange events over the past few days

and nodded. They never said so, but actions spoke louder than words. "Yes, I guess so. But still…"

"You're lucky to have them."

The sadness in his voice tugged at her heart. She reached across the space between them and covered his fist on the bench seat. He turned his hand over and opened it, lacing his fingers between hers. That simple gesture gave her hope. She clung to the feeling as they drove out of town.

He turned at a familiar fruit stand and she sat up straighter. "Are we going to the farm?"

"Yeah."

When they arrived, Rex rolled his motorcycle down a narrow metal ramp from the truck bed to the gravel driveway first and then repeated the action with a smaller bright blue bike. He reached into the saddlebag and withdrew an owner's manual. "Need to read it before we go for a ride?"

Her cheeks heated, but the tender smile on his lips curled her toes. "No."

He tucked the book away and handed her a set of keys and a helmet the same color as the bike. "This one works the same way as my bike, but weighs about half as much. Give 'er a try. We'll take a few slow laps around the farm."

Fear and excitement raced through her veins as she buckled the helmet and climbed on the motorcycle. Her hands trembled as she grasped the rubber handgrips and fired the engine. She had no idea what kind of game Rex was playing, but she'd play along just for the opportunity to be with him.

He led her around the perimeter of the land, glancing back frequently to check her progress. A sense of freedom filled Juliana as the wind whipped her shirttails and caressed her cheeks. No matter what happened after today, she would buy herself a motorcycle, and she would not revert back to the woman who'd let fear of disappointing her parents rule her life. It was *her* life and she intended to live every second of it from this moment forward.

She followed Rex through an open gate, and drove down a path and up a shallow rise. The freshly mowed grass smelled heavenly. When he stopped and killed the engine, she pulled alongside him and did the same. He removed his helmet and climbed from his machine. She mimicked his actions.

Why had he stopped here in the middle of this pasture?

"This is a good place for a house," he said.

"It's a beautiful site." Insects buzzed and not one single cloud marred the blue sky. A hundred yards away, fish splashed and ducks quacked in a small pond. Cattails waved in the breeze and lily pads dotted the water's surface.

"I'm buying the farm and I'm going to build right here." He pointed to the ground at his feet.

She jerked her gaze to his and found him watching her carefully. "You're not going back on tour?"

"No. Everyone I love is here."

"I'm sure Kelly and the girls will be thrilled."

"Will you?"

Her breath hitched. "Me?"

Rex cupped her shoulders. The look in his eyes weakened her knees and made her heart pound. Hope brought a lump to her throat.

"I love you, Juliana. I want to marry you and build a home with you. Right here." His spread his hand below her navel and then he rubbed in a slow circle. Desire curled beneath his palm. "I want to make babies with you."

She mashed her lips together and blinked furiously while she tried to make sense of his words. "Me?" she repeated.

"Yeah, you. I have a thing for good girls who want to be bad." His be-bad-with-me grin made her absolutely giddy with delight.

"I like being bad with you."

"Good. Because I feel like being bad right now and for the next fifty years or so." His hands tangled in her hair and then he took her mouth in a deep, soul-robbing kiss.

Juliana savored his taste, the slickness of his tongue and the heat of his breath on her cheek. She wriggled closer, winding her arms around his middle and fusing herself to the hot length of his body.

He lifted his head and tenderly stroked her cheeks. "I should have believed you when you told me about your mother and your childhood. But I'll never buy your story about being an unresponsive lover. Babe, you are the hottest woman I've ever known."

Pleasure percolated through her and a smart-aleck grin stretched her lips. "And you should know."

He winced. "I'm sorry for all the women who weren't you. And I swear to you that none of them excited me the way you do."

She cradled his jaw. "Don't be sorry, Rex. Your past is what made you the man I love."

He inhaled deeply and closed his eyes. His jaw muscles bunched. "Say it again."

The deep timber of his voice sent a tidal wave of longing through her. "I love you. *You,* my reluctant rebel."

He brushed back her hair. "And in case you're afraid your mother is right about me wanting your money—"

"I'm not."

"You don't have to be. My share of my inheritance from my parents was enough to pay off my loan and make a big down payment on this land. If I need to show your folks a financial statement—"

"You won't have to do that. You've already won my mother over. She was the tough sell."

She rose on her tiptoes and pressed her lips to his. His big hands cupped her buttocks, lifting and pressing her tightly against the solid ridge of his arousal. The kiss was long and slow and deep. She wanted to weep from the sheer eroticism of the way he made love to her mouth. And then his hands swept beneath her shirt. Rough skin abraded her waist.

She gasped, drew back and clasped his right hand in hers. Blisters in various stages of healing covered his fingertips. "What happened?"

He shrugged. "Loving you has filled me with music. I can't play as fast as my brain forms the lyrics and melodies."

His words touched her profoundly. Juliana pressed a hand to her heart. "I would never ask you to give that up. I meant what I said in your office. If you want to go back on the road, I'll quit my job and follow you anywhere."

He lifted her hand and kissed her knuckles. "You love your job. I don't want you to quit. I realized it's the songwriting I love. Not being onstage. Not the fans. Not the traveling. I can stay here with you, run Renegade and write songs for other people to sing. According to John Lee, my manager, I should make enough money to take care of you and any babies we make." His hand smoothed over her belly, stirring up a whirlpool of need.

He dropped to one knee in the grass and reached into his pocket. The diamond solitaire he pulled out flashed fire in the sunlight. It wasn't nearly as flashy as Wally's ring but it was ten times more beautiful. "Marry me, Juliana Alden. Let me love you forever."

Winding her arms around his neck, she slid down his body an inch at a time until she knelt with him in the grass and then she kissed him, pouring all of her love into the caress. His arms banded around her, holding her close. She lifted her lips a fraction of an inch and looked into the eyes of the man she loved.

"On one condition. You get rid of that crazy notion that you have to support me. I make good money, and I'm good at what I do. One of these days I may cut my hours to spend more time with our children, but this will always be a partnership. We'll take care of each other."

"Deal."

"Then yes, Rex Tanner, I'll marry you and spend forever with you. I can't think of anything more perfect than making music and babies with you."

Rex slid the ring onto her finger and Juliana grinned through happy tears. Forget nice. Forget boring. The adventure of a lifetime had just begun. She'd get to be bad whenever she wanted and it would be so good.

* * * * *

Don't miss Andrea's story in the next installment of
TRUST FUND AFFAIRS.
Watch for
EXPOSING THE EXECUTIVE'S SECRETS
in July 2006
from Silhouette Desire

HARLEQUIN®

Super Romance

THE PRODIGAL'S RETURN

by *Anna DeStefano*

Prom night for Jenn Gardner and Neal Cain turned
into a tragedy that tore them apart. Eight years
later, Jenn has made a life for herself and her young
daughter. But when Neal comes home, Jenn sees that
he is still consumed with the past. Maybe she can
convince him that he's paid enough and deserves
happiness a second time around.

"Anna DeStefano's remarkable stories of the healing
power of love touch the heart with hope. One of the
genre's rising stars..."
—Gayle Wilson, two-time
RITA® Award-winning author

On sale July 2006!
*Available wherever books are sold, including most
bookstores, supermarkets, discount stores and drugstores.*

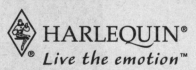

HARLEQUIN®
Live the emotion™

**Hidden in the secrets of antiquity,
lies the unimagined truth...**

Introducing

a brand-new line filled with mystery
and suspense, action and adventure,
and a fascinating look into history.

And it all begins with DESTINY.

In a sealed crypt in
France, where the
terrifying legend of
the beast of Gevaudan
begins to unravel,
Annja Creed discovers
a stunning artifact
that will seal her destiny.

*Available every other
month starting
July 2006, wherever
you buy books.*

GRA1

Baseball. The crack of the bat,
the roar of the crowd…and the view
of mouthwatering men in tight uniforms!
A sport in which the men are men…
and the women are drooling.

Join three Blaze bestselling authors in
celebrating the men who indulge in this
all-American pastime—and the women
who help them indulge in other things….

Boys of Summer

A Hot (and Sweaty!)
Summer Collection

*One book,
three great
stories!*

FEVER PITCH
by Julie Elizabeth Leto
THE SWEET SPOT by Kimberly Raye
SLIDING HOME by Leslie Kelly

On sale this July
Feel the heat. Get your copy today!

www.eHarlequin.com   HBBOSJUL

If you enjoyed what you just read,
then we've got an offer you can't resist!

Take 2 bestselling
love stories FREE!

Plus get a FREE surprise gift!

Clip this page and mail it to Silhouette Reader Service™

IN U.S.A.	IN CANADA
3010 Walden Ave.	P.O. Box 609
P.O. Box 1867	Fort Erie, Ontario
Buffalo, N.Y. 14240-1867	L2A 5X3

YES! Please send me 2 free Silhouette Desire® novels and my free surprise gift. After receiving them, if I don't wish to receive anymore, I can return the shipping statement marked cancel. If I don't cancel, I will receive 6 brand-new novels every month, before they're available in stores! In the U.S.A., bill me at the bargain price of $3.80 plus 25¢ shipping and handling per book and applicable sales tax, if any*. In Canada, bill me at the bargain price of $4.47 plus 25¢ shipping and handling per book and applicable taxes**. That's the complete price and a savings of at least 10% off the cover prices—what a great deal! I understand that accepting the 2 free books and gift places me under no obligation ever to buy any books. I can always return a shipment and cancel at any time. Even if I never buy another book from Silhouette, the 2 free books and gift are mine to keep forever.

225 SDN DZ9F
326 SDN DZ9G

Name	(PLEASE PRINT)	
Address	Apt.#	
City	State/Prov.	Zip/Postal Code

Not valid to current Silhouette Desire® subscribers.

Want to try two free books from another series?
Call 1-800-873-8635 or visit www.morefreebooks.com.

* Terms and prices subject to change without notice. Sales tax applicable in N.Y.
** Canadian residents will be charged applicable provincial taxes and GST.
All orders subject to approval. Offer limited to one per household.
® are registered trademarks owned and used by the trademark owner and or its licensee.

DES04R   ©2004 Harlequin Enterprises Limited

Coming in July 2006

The NEW Destination for Romance

Love's Ultimate Destination

FOUR NEW TITLES
EVERY MONTH FROM
AUTHORS YOU KNOW AND LOVE

Visit Kimani Romance at www.kimanipress.com

KRLOGO

COMING NEXT MONTH

SDCNM0606